My Fathers' Ghost Is Climbing in the Rain

My Fathers' Ghost Is Climbing in the Rain

PATRICIO PRON

Translated from the Spanish by
MARA FAYE LETHEM

ALFRED A. KNOPF · NEW YORK · 2013

THIS IS A BORZOI BOOK
PUBLISHED BY ALFRED A. KNOPF

Translation copyright © 2013 by Mara Faye Lethem
All rights reserved. Published in the United States by Alfred A. Knopf,
a division of Random House, Inc., New York, and in Canada
by Random House of Canada Limited, Toronto. Originally published
in Spain as *El espíritu de mis padres sigue subiendo en la lluvia*
by Random House Mondadori, S. A., Barcelona, in 2011.
Copyright © 2011 by Patricio Pron. This translation originally published
in the United Kingdom by Faber & Faber Limited, London.
www.aaknopf.com

Grateful acknowledgment is made to the following for
permission to reprint previously published material:

Bob Dylan Music Company: Excerpt from "I Want You" by Bob Dylan,
copyright © 1966 by Dwarf Music, renewed 1994 by Dwarf Music.
Reprinted by permission of Bob Dylan Music Company.

New Directions Publishing Corporation: Excerpt from
"Thou Shalt Not Kill" by Kenneth Rexroth, from *Selected Poems,*
copyright © 1956 by Kenneth Rexroth. Reprinted by permission of
New Directions Publishing Corp.

Library of Congress Cataloging-in-Publication Data
Pron, Patricio, [date]
[Espíritu de mis padres sigue subiendo en la lluvia, English]
My fathers' ghost is climbing in the rain / by Patricio Pron ;
translated from the Spanish by Mara Faye Lethem. —
First American edition.
pages cm
ISBN 978-0-307-70068-1 (alk. paper)
I. Lethem, Mara, translator. II. Title.
PQ7798.26.R58E8713 2013
863'.64—dc22   2012049209

Front-of-jacket image: Photos.com / Jupiterimages
Jacket design by Carol Devine Carson

Manufactured in the United States of America
First American Edition

They are murdering all the young men.
For half a century now, every day,
They have hunted them down and killed them.
They are killing them now.
At this minute, all over the world,
They are killing the young men.
They know ten thousand ways to kill them.
Every year they invent new ones.

Kenneth Rexroth, "Thou Shalt Not Kill:
A Memorial for Dylan Thomas"

I

The true story of what I saw and how I saw it [. . .] is after all the only thing I've got to offer.

—Jack Kerouac

1

Between March or April 2000 and August 2008, while I was traveling and writing articles and living in Germany, my consumption of certain drugs made me almost completely lose my memory, so that what I remember of those eight years—at least what I remember of some ninety-five months of those eight years—is pretty vague and sketchy: I remember the rooms of two houses I lived in, I remember snow getting in my shoes as I struggled to make my way to the street from the door of one of those houses, I remember that later I spread salt and the snow turned brown and started to dissolve, I remember the door to the office of the psychiatrist who treated me but I don't remember his name or how I found him. He was balding and weighed me on every visit; I guess it was once a month or something like that. He asked me how things were going, and then he weighed me and gave me more pills. A few years after leaving that German city, I returned and retraced the path to that psychiatrist's office and I read his name on the plaque alongside the other doorbells, but it was just a name, nothing that explained why I'd visited him or why he'd weighed me each time, or how I could have let my memory go down the drain like

3

that; at the time, I told myself I could knock on his door and ask him why I'd been his patient and what had happened to me during those years, but then I thought I should have made an appointment, that the psychiatrist wouldn't remember me anyway, and, besides, I'm not really all that curious about myself. Maybe one day a child of mine will want to know who his father was and what he did during those eight years in Germany and he'll go to the city and walk through it, and, perhaps, with his father's directions, he'll show up at the psychiatrist's office and find out everything. I suppose at some point all children need to know who their parents were and they take it upon themselves to find out. Children are detectives of their parents, who cast them out into the world so that one day the children will return and tell them their story so that they themselves can understand it. These children aren't judging their parents—it's impossible for them to be truly impartial, since they owe them everything, including their lives—but they can try to impose some order on their story, restore the meaning that gets stripped away by the petty events of life and their accumulation, and then they can protect that story and perpetuate it in their memory. Children are policemen of their parents, but I don't like policemen. They've never gotten along well with my family.

4

My father and I hadn't spoken in some time. It wasn't anything personal, I just didn't usually have a telephone on hand when I wanted to talk to him and he didn't have anywhere to call me if he ever wanted to. A few months before he got sick, I left the room I'd been renting in that German city and started sleeping on the couches of people I knew. I didn't do it because I was broke, but for the feeling of irresponsibility that I assumed came with not having a home or obligations, with leaving everything behind. And honestly it wasn't bad, but the problem is, when you live like that you can't have many possessions, so gradually I parted with my books, with the few objects I'd bought since arriving in Germany and with my clothes; all I held on to were some shirts, because I discovered that a clean shirt can open doors for you when you have nowhere to go. I usually washed them by hand in the morning while I showered and then let them dry inside one of the lockers at the library in the literature department of the university where I worked, or on the grass in a park where I used to go to kill time before searching out the hospitality and companionship of the owner of some sofa. I was just passing through.

5

Sometimes I couldn't sleep; when that happened, I'd get up off the sofa and walk toward my host's bookshelves, always different but also always, without fail, located beside the sofa, as if reading were possible only in the perpetual discomfort of that piece of furniture in which one is neither properly seated nor completely stretched out. Then I would look at the books and think how I used to read them one right after the next but how at that point they left me completely cold. On those bookshelves there were almost never books by those dead writers I'd read when I was a poor teenager in a poor neighborhood of a poor city in a poor country, and I was stupidly insistent on becoming part of that imaginary republic to which they belonged, a republic with vague borders in which writers wrote in New York or in London, in Berlin or in Buenos Aires, and yet I wasn't of that world. I had wanted to be like them, and the only proof that remained of that determination, and the resolve that came with it, was that trip to Germany, the country where the writers that most interested me had lived and had died and, above all, had written, and a fistful of books that already belonged to a literature I had tried and failed to escape; a literature like the nightmare of a dying writer, or, better yet, of a dying, talentless Argentine writer; of a writer, let's say, who is not the author of *The Aleph,* around whom we all inevitably revolve, but rather the author of *On Heroes and Tombs,* someone who spent his whole life believing that he was talented and important and morally unquestionable and who at the very end discovers that he's completely without talent and behaved ridiculously and brunched with dictators, and then he feels ashamed and wants his country's literature to be at the level of his miserable body of work so that it wasn't written in vain and might even have one or two followers. Well, I had been part of that literature, and every time I thought about it, it was as if in my head an old man was shouting *Tornado! Tornado!* announcing the end of days, as in a Mexican film I had once seen; except that the days had kept coming and I had been able to grab onto the trunks of those trees that remained standing in the tornado only by quitting writing, completely quitting writing and reading, and by seeing books for what they were, the only thing that I'd ever been able to call my home, but complete strangers in that time of pills and vivid dreams in which I no longer remembered nor wanted to remember what a damn home was.

6

Once, when I was a boy, I asked my mother to buy me a box of toys that—though I didn't know it at the time—came from Germany and were made close to a place where I would live in the future. The box contained an adult woman, a shopping cart, two boys, a girl and a dog, but it had no adult man and was, as the representation of a family—since that's what it was—incomplete. I didn't know it then, but I had wanted my mother to give me a family, even if it was just a toy one, and my mother had been able to give me only an incomplete family, a family without a father; once again, a family vulnerable to the elements. I had then taken a toy Roman soldier and stripped him of his armor and turned him into the father of that toy family, but I didn't know how to play with them, I had no idea what families did, and the family that my mother had given me ended up in the back of a closet, the five characters looking at each other and perhaps shrugging their toy shoulders in the face of their ignorance of their roles, as if forced to represent an ancient civilization whose monuments and cities had not yet been unearthed by archeologists and whose language remained undeciphered.

7

Something had happened to my parents and to me and to my siblings that prevented me from ever knowing what a home was or what a family was, though everything seemed to indicate I had both. Many times in the past I had tried to understand what that thing had been, but then and there, in Germany, I stopped trying, like someone who accepts the mutilations from a car accident he can't remember. My parents and I had that accident: something crossed our path and our car spun around a few times and went off the highway, and we were now wandering through the fields, our minds blank, that shared experience the only thing uniting us. Behind us there was an overturned car in a ditch on the side of a country road, bloodstains on the seats and in the grass, but none of us wanted to turn around and look back.

9

As I flew toward my father, toward something I didn't know but that was disgusting and frightening and sad, I wanted to remember what I could about

my life with him. There wasn't much: I remembered
my father building our house; I remembered him
coming home from one of the newspapers where
he worked with a noise of papers and keys and a
scent of tobacco; I remembered him once hugging
my mother and many times sleeping with a book in
his hands, which always, as my father nodded off,
dropped to cover his face as if he were a dead man
found on the street during some war; and I could
also remember him often driving, looking forward
with a frown at a road that was either straight or
sinuous and located in the provinces of Santa Fe,
Córdoba, La Rioja, Catamarca, Entre Ríos, Buenos
Aires, all those provinces through which my father
took us in an attempt to show us their beauty—
a beauty I found hard to grasp—always trying to
give meaning to those symbols we learned in a
school that had yet to cast off a dictatorship whose
values it continued to perpetuate. Symbols that
children like me would draw using a plastic stencil
our mothers bought for us, with which, if you ran a
pencil over the lines cut into the plastic, you could
draw a house that we were told was in Tucumán,
another building that was in Buenos Aires, a round
cockade and a flag that was sky blue and white,
which we knew well because it was supposedly
our flag, although we had seen it so many times in
circumstances that weren't really ours, completely
beyond our control, circumstances that we didn't
have anything to do with and didn't want to have

maybe even me. Where do I live, said my father again, and the other person—my mother, or one of my siblings, or maybe even me—recited the address; a little while later he was home, sitting at the table reading a newspaper as if nothing had happened or as if he'd forgotten what had happened. Another time, someone rang the bell; my father, who was closest, grabbed the intercom near the kitchen and asked who it was. We are Jehovah's Witnesses, they said. Whose witnesses, asked my father. Jehovah's, they answered. And what do you want, my father asked again. We come to bring you the word of God, they said. Of who, asked my father. The word of God, they said. My father asked again: Who. We are Jehovah's Witnesses, they said. Whose witnesses, asked my father. Jehovah's, they answered. And what do you want, my father asked again. We come to bring you the word of God, they said. Of who, asked my father. The word of God, they answered. No, they brought me that last week, said my father, and he hung up without even glancing at me, beside him and looking perplexed. Then he walked over to my mother and asked her where the newspaper was. On the stove, replied my mother, and neither she nor I told him that he was the one who'd left it there a few minutes earlier.

11

I used to think my father's bad memory was just an excuse to get him out of the few inconveniences caused by a daily life that he'd long ago left in my mother's hands: birthdays, anniversaries, groceries. If my father had carried a date book, I'd thought, it would have been one in which the pages of the following day fell out, an object always in flames like a pyromaniac's diary. I'd thought it was all a trick my father had come up with, his way of avoiding things that for some reason were too much for him, among which were me and my brother and sister but also a past that I'd barely glimpsed—childhood in a small town, an interrupted political career, years of working at newspapers that were like those boxers who spend more time on the mat than standing and fighting, a political past that I thought I knew nothing about and that maybe I didn't want to know about—which didn't lead me to suspect who my father really was, the abyss he had faced and how he'd barely gotten out of it alive. When I spoke with my sister at the hospital, though, I realized that something had always been wrong with my father and that maybe his lack of memory wasn't faked, and I also realized that I had come to this discovery too late, too late for me and too late for him, and that's how it always happens, even though it's sad to say so.

12

Actually, there was another memory, although it wasn't a direct recollection, something that had come from experience and had lodged in the mind, but rather something that I had seen in my parents' house, a photograph. In it, my father and I are sitting on a small stone wall; behind us, an abyss and, a bit beyond, mountains and hills that—though the photograph is in black and white—one imagines green and red and brown. My father and I are sitting on the wall like this: he, in profile, with his arms crossed; I, with my back to the abyss, and my hands beneath my thighs. Looking carefully at the photograph, one will see that it has a certain dramatic intensity not attributable to the landscape—though it is dramatic in the way that some people imagine a landscape can be—but rather to the relationship between us. My father is looking at the landscape; I am looking at him, and in my gaze there is a very specific plea: that he notice me, that he take me down off that wall where my legs hang without touching the ground and which seems to me—inevitably an exaggeration, because I'm just a boy—about to collapse at any moment and drag me into the abyss along with it. In the photograph, my father doesn't look at me; he doesn't even notice that I am looking at him or acknowledge the entreaty I was capable of formulating only in that way, as if he and I were doomed not to understand each other, not to even see each other. My father in the photograph has the hair I'm going to have, the same torso I'll have in the future, now, when I am older than he was when someone—my mother, probably—took that photograph of us as we climbed a mountain whose name I don't recall. Perhaps at that moment, as I thought about him, as I sat on an airplane, he felt for me the fear I had felt then on a mountain in the province of La Rioja around 1983 or 1984. However, as I traveled in that airplane back to a country that my father loved and that was also mine, a country that for me was just like the abyss he and I had posed in front of, not understanding each other, for a photograph, I didn't yet know that my father knew fear much better than I thought, that my father had lived with it and fought against it and, like everyone, had lost that battle in a silent war that had been his and his entire generation's.

13

I hadn't been back to that country for eight years, but when the airplane dropped into the airport and spat us out, I felt as if it had been even longer. I'd once heard that the minutes spent on a roller coaster were, as perceived by the people in the car, longer than the ones spent at the foot of the ride watching others scream and grip the metal bar, and in that moment I had the impression that the country itself had gotten on a roller coaster and continued twisting upside down as if the operator had gone crazy or was on his lunch break. I saw old young people who wore clothes that were both old and new at the same time, I saw a blue carpet that looked new but was already dirty and worn where it had been stepped on, I saw some booths with yellow glass panes and some young but old policemen who looked distrustingly at passports and sometimes stamped them and sometimes didn't; even my passport already looked old and, when they gave it back to me, I felt as if they were handing me a dead plant beyond any hope of being brought back to life; I saw a young woman in a miniskirt giving passersby cookies made with dulce de leche, and I could almost see the dust of the years settled on those cookies and in the caramel. She said to me: Would you like to try a cookie? And I shook my head and practically ran toward the exit. As I left, I thought I saw the old, obese caricature of a soccer player, and I thought I saw him being chased by dozens of photographers and journalists and that the soccer player wore a T-shirt printed with an old photograph of himself, a photograph monstrously disfigured by his belly that showed an exaggeratedly large leg, a curved, elongated torso and an enormous hand hitting a ball to score a goal in some World Cup on any old day of some springtime past.

14

But maybe that didn't really happen and it was all a hallucination induced by the pills that doctor gave me and I silently swallowed on the sofas of people I knew in that German city. Once, long after all that happened, I reread the instructions on one of those medications, which I'd read so many times before but nevertheless had forgotten every time. I read that those pills had a sedative, antidepressive and tranquilizing effect. I read that they took effect between one and six hours after being taken orally but that eliminating them required some one hundred and twenty hours—which makes five days, according to my calculations—and eighty-eight percent passes through urine and seven percent through sweat, and five percent of the substance is never eliminated. I read that it produces physical and psychological dependence and that it induces amnesia as well as a decrease in or a complete lack of ability to remember events that take place during the periods of the drug's effectiveness. I read that it can cause suicidal tendencies in the patient—which is, undoubtedly, serious; drowsiness—which is, of course, not; weakness; fatigue; disorientation; ataxia; nausea; emotional blunting; reduced alertness; loss of appetite or of weight; sleepiness; breathlessness; double vision; sleep disturbances; dizziness; vomiting; headaches; sexual disturbances; depersonalization; hyperacusia; numbness or tingling in extremities; hypersensitivity to light or physical contact; hallucinations or epileptic convulsions; respiratory, gastrointestinal or muscular problems; increase in hostility or irritability; anterograde amnesia; alteration of the perception of reality and mental confusion; slurred speech; abnormalities in liver and kidney function; and withdrawal symptoms following abrupt discontinuation of the medication. So I guess seeing a soccer player wearing a T-shirt with a deformed image of his own past over his gut is among the least serious things that can happen to you when you take stuff like that.

15

Anyway, that encounter, which really happened and which, therefore, was true, can be read here simply as an invention, as something fake, since, first of all, I was sufficiently confused at the time and so clearly worried that I could and did distrust my senses, which could incorrectly interpret a real event, and, second, because that encounter with the aging soccer player from a country that was part of my past, and almost everything that happened later, which I'm here to explain, was true but not necessarily believable. It has been said that in literature the beautiful is true but the true in literature is only the believable, and between the believable and the true there is a vast distance. Not to mention the beautiful, which is something that should never be discussed: the beautiful should be literature's nature preserve, the place where beauty prospers without literature's hand ever touching it, and it should serve to entertain and console writers, since literature and beauty are completely different things or perhaps the same thing, like two gloves for the right hand. Except you can't put a right-hand glove on your left hand; some things don't go together. I had just arrived in Argentina, and while I waited for the bus that would take me to the city where my parents lived, almost two hundred miles to the northeast of Buenos Aires, I was thinking that I had come from the dark German forests to the horizontal Argentine plain to see my father die and to say good-bye to him and to promise him—even though I didn't believe it in the slightest—that he and I were going to have another chance, in some other place, for each of us to discover who the other was and that, perhaps, for the first time since he had become a father and I a son, we would finally understand something; but this, being true, wasn't the least bit believable.

18

And then there was the impossible tongue twister of the ill and their doctors, who brought together words like *benzodiazepine, diazepam, neuroleptic, hypnotic, zolpidem, tranquilizer, alprazolam, narcotic, antiepileptic, antihistamine, clonazepam, barbiturate, lorazepam, triazolobenzodiazepine, escitalopram—* all words amid the jumbled words in a head that refused to function.

20

When I got to my parents' house, nobody was there. The house was cold and damp, like a fish whose belly, as a boy, I had once brushed against before throwing it back into the water. It didn't feel like my house—that old sensation that a particular place is your home had vanished forever—and I was afraid the house would consider my presence an insult. I didn't touch even a single chair: I left my small suitcase in the entryway and I began to walk through the rooms, like a snoop. In the kitchen there was a hunk of bread that some ants had started eating. Someone had left a change of clothes and an open empty handbag on my parents' bed. The bed was unmade and the sheets retained the shape of a body that perhaps was my mother's. Beside it, on my father's night table, there was a book that I didn't look at, some eyeglasses and two or three bottles of pills. When I saw them, I told myself that my father and I had something in common after all, that he and I were still tied to life by the invisible threads of pills and prescriptions and that those threads also now somehow united us. My old room was on the other side of the hallway. As I went into it, I thought everything must have shrunk: that the table was smaller than I remembered it, that the chair beside it could be used only by a midget, that the windows were tiny and that there weren't as many books as I remembered, and besides they'd been written by authors who no longer interested me. It seemed as if I'd been gone more than eight years, I thought as I lay on what had been my bed. I was cold but I didn't want to cover myself with the bedspread, and I lay there, with one arm over my face, unable to sleep but also unwilling to stand up, thinking in circles about my father and about me and about a lost opportunity for him and for me and for all of us.

21

My mother came into the kitchen and found me contemplating the products in the refrigerator. Like those dreams in which everything is suspiciously familiar and at the same time shockingly strange, the products were the same but their containers had changed, and now the beans were in a can that reminded me of the old tomato can, the tomatoes came in a canister that reminded me of the cocoa and the cocoa came in bags that made me think of diapers and sleepless nights. My mother didn't seem at all affected by my presence, but I was surprised to see her so thin and so fragile; when I stood up and she came over to hug me, I saw she had a gaze that could turn the demons out of hell, and I wondered if that gaze wasn't enough to cure my father, to alleviate the pain and suffering of all the patients in the hospital where he lay dying, because that gaze was the gaze of a will that can stand up to anything. What happened, I asked my mother, and she started to explain, slowly. When she finished, she went to her room to cry alone and I put some water and a fistful of rice into a pot and I stared through the window at the impenetrable jungle that had grown from the garden my mother and brother had tended so carefully, in the same place but in a different time.

23

My siblings were standing in the hallway when I arrived at the hospital. From a distance they seemed silent, although later I saw that they were talking or pretending to, as if they felt obligated to simulate keeping up a conversation that not even they were really listening to. My sister started to cry when she saw me, as if I were bringing terrible and unexpected news, or as if I myself were that news, returning horribly mutilated from a never-ending war. I handed them some chocolates and a bottle of schnapps that I'd bought in Germany, in the airport, and my sister started laughing and crying at the same time.

24

My father was lying beneath a tangle of cords like a fly in a spiderweb. His hand was cold and my face was hot, but I noticed that only when I brought my hand to my face to wipe it.

25

I stayed with him that evening, without really knowing what to do except look at him and ask myself what would happen if he opened his eyes or spoke, and for a moment I hoped that he wouldn't open them while I was there. Then I said to myself: I'm going to close my eyes and count to ten and when I open them none of this will be real, it will never have happened, like when films end or you close a book; but when I opened my eyes, after having counted to ten, my father was still there and I was still there and the spiderweb was still there, and we were all surrounded by the noises of the hospital and that heavy air that smells of disinfectant and false hopes and is sometimes worse than sickness or death. Have you ever been in a hospital? Well, then you've seen them all. Have you watched someone die? It's different every time. Sometimes the illness is blinding and you close your eyes and what you most fear is like a car coming toward you at top speed along a country road some ordinary night. When I opened my eyes again, my sister was beside me and it was nighttime and my father was still alive, fighting and losing but still alive.

26

My sister insisted on spending the night at the hospital. I went back to the house with my brother and my mother and we watched a movie on television for a while. In the movie, a man ran through an intense snowstorm along a frozen track that seemed endless; the snow fell on his face and on his coat and sometimes it seemed to obstruct the man's vision of what he was chasing, but the man kept running as if his life depended on catching the airplane that taxied in front of him. *Johnny! Johnny!* shouted a woman who emerged from the open hatch of the airplane, which seemed about to take off at any minute. When the man was just about to reach her outstretched hand, however, the plane took off and another man violently snatched

house had changed, I had to be capable of comparing my way of seeing things in that moment and my way of seeing them before leaving and living in Germany and starting to take pills and before my father got sick and I came back, which was impossible. I distracted myself by looking at the books on the shelves in the living room, which were my parents' books from when they were young, in the light that entered from the street through a window. Although I knew those books well, perhaps it was also my perception that made them seem new to my eyes, and once again I wondered what had really changed from the time I'd flipped through them to now, when I looked at them without curiosity and with some apprehension in the light that filtered in from outside, and again I arrived at no conclusion. I was there for a while longer, standing on the cold floor of the living room, looking at those books. I heard a bus pass and then the cars of the first people headed to work, and I thought the city was soon going to set into motion again and I didn't want to be there to see it. I went to my room and took two more pills, and then I lay down in bed and waited for them to take effect; but, as always, I didn't really notice when they did, because first my legs went numb and then I could no longer move my arms and I merely managed to think about that slow falling to pieces that was the only way sleep came and to tell myself, a moment before finally drifting off, that I had to make lists of everything I saw, that I had to make an inventory of everything I was seeing in my parents' house so that I wouldn't forget it again. Then I fell asleep.

29

Titles found in my parents' library: *Another Episode in the Class War; Argentine Literature and Political Reality from Sarmiento to Cortázar; Around the Day in Eighty Worlds; Blade, Dull Edge and Point; British Policy in the River Plate Region; Collected Fictions; Diary of Che Guevara, The; Evita: In My Own Words; Folk Songbook; Foundation for National Reconstruction; Industry, Industrial Bourgeoisie and National Liberation; It Is the People's Time; Latin America, Now or Never; Life and Death of López Jordán; Little Red Book, The; Martín Fierro; Might Is the Right of Beasts; Mordisquito; My Life for Perón!; Nationalism and Liberation; Navigation Notebook; Operation Massacre; Organized Community, The; Perón, Man of Destiny; Peronism and Socialism; Peronist Doctrine; Peronist Philosophy; Perón Speaks: Speeches and Addresses of Juan Perón; Political Leadership; Prophets of Hate, Revolution and Counterrevolution in Argentina; Rosas, Our Contemporary; Satanovsky Case, The; Tactical Manual; What Is to Be Done?; Who Killed Rosendo?.* Authors found in my parents' library: Borges, Jorge Luis; Chávez,

Fermín; Cortázar, Julio; Duarte de Perón, Eva; Guevara, Ernesto; Hernández Arregui, Juan José; Jauretche, Arturo; Lenin, Vladimir Ilyich; Marechal, Leopoldo; Pavón Pereyra, Enrique; Peña, Milcíades; Perón, Juan Domingo; Ramos, Jorge Abelardo; Rosa, José María; Sandino, Augusto César; Santos Discépolo, Enrique; Scalabrini Ortiz, Raúl; Vigo, Juan M.; Viñas, David; Walsh, Rodolfo; Zedong, Mao. Authors absent from my parents' library: Bullrich, Silvina; Guido, Beatriz; Martínez Estrada, Ezequiel; Ocampo, Victoria; Sábato, Ernesto. Predominant colors of the covers of the books in my parents' library: sky blue, white and red. Most common publishing houses in their library: Plus Ultra, A. Peña Lillo, Freeland and Eudeba. Words that presumably most frequently appear in the books in my parents' library: *tactic, strategy, struggle, Argentina, Perón, revolution*. General condition of the books in my parents' library: poor, and in some cases terrible, dreadful or critical.

30

Once again: my parents haven't read Silvina Bullrich, Beatriz Guido, Ezequiel Martínez Estrada, Victoria Ocampo or Ernesto Sábato. They've read Jorge Luis Borges, Rodolfo Walsh and Leopoldo Marechal but not Silvina Bullrich, Beatriz Guido,

Ezequiel Martínez Estrada, Victoria Ocampo and Ernesto Sábato. They've read Ernesto Guevara, Eva and Juan Domingo Perón and Arturo Jauretche but not Silvina Bullrich, Beatriz Guido, Ezequiel Martínez Estrada, Victoria Ocampo and Ernesto Sábato. What's more: they've read Juan José Hernández Arregui, Jorge Abelardo Ramos and Enrique Pavón Pereyra but not Silvina Bullrich, Beatriz Guido, Ezequiel Martínez Estrada, Victoria Ocampo and Ernesto Sábato. One could spend hours thinking about this.

32

At first I took paroxetine and benzodiazepines, no more than fifteen milligrams; but fifteen milligrams was like a sneeze in a hurricane for me, something insignificant and without any effect, like trying to cover the sun with one hand or teach justice in the land of the reprobates, and so the dosage had gotten incrementally upped until it reached sixty milligrams, when there was nothing stronger on the market and the doctors looked the way the caravan leaders in Westerns look when they say they will go only that far because beyond is Comanche territory, and then they turn around and spur on their horses, but first they look at the members of the caravan and they know they'll never see them again and they feel shame and pity. Then I started to take sleeping pills too; when I took them, I fell into a state that must be like death, and through my mind passed words like *stomach, lamp* and *albino,* without any apparent connection. Sometimes I jotted them down the next morning, if I remembered them, but when I read them it was like flipping through the newspaper of a country sadder than the Sudan or Ethiopia, a country for which I had no visa nor did I want one, and I thought I heard a fire truck come barreling to put out the fucking flames of hell with a tank filled with gasoline.

35

A doctor started to walk toward us from the opposite end of the hallway, and when we saw him we stood up without thinking. I'm going to examine him, he warned us, and then he went into my father's room and he was there for a little while. We were waiting outside, not knowing what to say. My mother was looking out the large window behind us as a small tugboat dragged a much larger vessel upriver, toward the port. I held in my hands a magazine about cars, even though I don't know how to drive; someone had left it on one of the seats and I merely let my eyes slide over its pages in an exercise as restful as contemplating a landscape, although in this case it was a landscape of incomprehensible technological innovations. The doctor finally came out and said that everything was the same, that there was no news at all. I thought one of us should ask him something so that the doctor would see we were really worried about my father's situation, so I asked him how his temperature was. The doctor squinted for a second, and then he looked at me incredulously and stammered: His temperature is perfectly normal, there's no problem with his temperature; and I thanked him and he nodded and started to head down the hallway.

36

That morning my sister told me she'd once found a sentence underlined in a book that my father had left at her house. My sister showed me the book. The sentence was: "I have fought the good fight, I have finished the race: I have kept the faith." It was verse seven of chapter four of Paul's second letter to Timothy. Reading it, I thought that my father had underlined that sentence so it would inspire and console him, and perhaps also as an epitaph, and I thought that if I knew who I was, if the fog that was the pills dissipated for a moment so that I could know who I was, I would have wanted that epitaph for myself too, but then I thought that I hadn't really fought, and that no one in my generation had fought; something or someone had already inflicted a defeat on us and we drank or took pills or wasted time in a thousand and one ways as a mode of hastening an end, possibly an undignified one but liberating nonetheless. Nobody had fought, we had all lost and barely anyone had stayed true to what they believed, whatever that was, I thought; my father's generation had been different, but, once again, there was something in that difference that was also a meeting point, a thread that went through the years and brought us together in spite of everything and was horrifically Argentine: the feeling of parents and children being united in defeat.

38

My mother started to prepare a meal and I went to help her, getting up from watching the television my brother had muted. While I peeled the onions, I thought that the recipe, in its glorious simplicity of bygone eras, would soon be lost in a period of confusion and stupidity, and I told myself that I should at least save it—since perpetuating that moment of shared happiness, perhaps one of the last with my mother before I returned to Germany, was impossible. I thought I had to perpetuate that recipe before it was too late. I grabbed a pen and started to take notes so I wouldn't forget that moment, but all I could do was write down the recipe; a simple, short recipe, yet relevant to me as a relic of a time of procedures, of a time of precise and punctuated steps, so different from those days of pain that blunted us all.

39

So this is the recipe: Take a good amount of ground beef, spread it over a cotton dish towel, distribute diced onions and chopped olives over the meat, along with hard-boiled eggs and anything else you want to add—here the options seem limitless: pieces of pepper, raisins, dried apricots or prunes, almonds, walnuts, hazelnuts, canned vegetables, et cetera—and then knead the meat so that the ingredients you've added are well distributed throughout. Then season with salt, paprika, cumin and chili powder and use the dish towel to shape the meat into a compact block that doesn't break apart as you handle it; if the meat doesn't stick together well, you can add bread crumbs. When the mixture is ready, place it into a lightly oiled mold and put it in the oven. Bake it until the meat loaf—since that's what you're making—is golden brown. It can be eaten hot or cold and accompanied by a salad.

42

The doctor—perhaps the one from before or maybe a different one; they all look the same to me—said: Anything can happen. And in my head those three words kept turning around until they had no meaning: Anything can happen, anything can happen, anything can happen, anything can happen, anything can happen, anything can happen . . .

45

My brother was nervously flipping channels until he stopped on one. It was showing a war film. Even though the plot was confusing and the acting was horrible and constantly thwarted by a camera that seemed to have been deliberately placed where the characters' faces couldn't be seen or where they should be walking, which brought about inevitable cuts where presumably the actors tripped over the camera and they had to redo the take, I slowly understood that the film was about a man who, after an accident, which wasn't shown dead or had moved, and another two agreed to talk to him only to admit they didn't know who he was or why their names appeared on that list; on both occasions the conversation was tense and ended badly, with the protagonist getting thrown out. He wasn't surprised that all of the people on his list were somehow related to the hospital. The one remaining person refused to talk to him, so the protagonist started to hang around his house. He discovered with some surprise that he had a huge talent for spying, a talent that allowed him to observe people without being seen and to blend into the crowd when he was being followed. An incidental talent, which he discovered one night, was picking locks; after opening one, he entered a dark room, some sort of poorly lit living room; he advanced silently a few steps and headed toward an adjacent room that, he discovered, was the kitchen; when he retraced his steps back toward the living room, he felt a blow from above and fell to the floor facedown. As he turned over, he received another blow, this time on the shoulder, and fell again, but just then he discovered a floor lamp in reach and switched it on: light bathed the room for an instant and his attacker, blinded, stepped back. Then the protagonist grabbed the lamp and dealt him a blow to the head. In the path traced through the air by the lamp on its way to the attacker's head, and before the cord was pulled out of the outlet, the protagonist was able to see that his attacker was tall and sickly-looking. The attacker's face was familiar, even on the floor, with his head bleeding; the protagonist turned on a small lamp that was on a table and, as he brought it closer to the face of his opponent, who looked dead and maybe really was, the protagonist discovered that he was that doctor from whom the nurse often protected him. As in most bad films—and this one really was bad, which I think had been clear to me from the beginning—the protagonist's sequence of thoughts was visually represented by the repetition of previous scenes: the face of the nurse who looked like a butcher; her antagonism toward the head doctor, which she covered up with deference; the handing over of the list and the money; the meetings with some of the people on the list, almost all of them doctors and almost all employees of the hospital where he had been treated after his accident. And there was one more scene, which had not been shown previously and which, given that the protagonist could not have been present—or, having been present during his convalescence, he must not have understood or couldn't remember—was only speculation: the nurse writing the list with a smile on her contorted face. At that moment, the viewer understood that the protagonist had been used by the nurse who looked like a butcher to get rid of those people she didn't want around or who had at some point humiliated or hurt her, and he understood that

I learned to read on my own at five years old; I read dozens of books, but I no longer remember anything about them except that they were written by foreign authors who were dead. That a writer could be Argentine and living is a fairly recent discovery and still shocks me. My mother says I didn't cry during my first days of life; mainly what I did was sleep. My mother says when I was a baby, my head was so big that if they left me sitting, I would start to sway and then fall headfirst toward one side or the other. I remember crying several times as a child, but I haven't cried since the death of my paternal grandfather in 1993 or 1994, presumably because the medication doesn't allow me to. Perhaps the only real effect of the pills is that they hinder complete happiness or complete sadness; it's like floating in a pool without ever seeing its bottom but not being able to reach the surface. I lost my virginity at fifteen; I don't know how many women I've had sex with since then. I ran away from the day care my mother took me to when I was three years old; in the reconstruction of the time that passed between my disappearance and when I was turned in to a police station, there are one hundred minutes in which nobody knows where I was, not even me. My paternal grandfather was a painter, my maternal grandfather worked on trains; the former was an anarchist and the latter a Peronist, I think. My paternal grandfather once pissed on the flagpole of a police station, but I don't know why or when; I think I remember it was because they didn't let him vote or something like that. My maternal grandfather was a guard who worked the line from Córdoba to Rosario; before that, the train passed through Jujuy and Salta and then on to Buenos Aires, where it ended; this was the trajectory that carried the explosives used by the Peronist Resistance, but even though their transportation wasn't possible without the collaboration of train employees, I don't know if my grandfather was an active collaborator. I don't remember the first record I bought, but I remember I heard the first song that moved me inside a car in a place called Candonga, in the province of Córdoba; actually, they were two songs on a radio program that came through the mountains, which distorted the sound and made it seem broadcast straight from the past. My father didn't like Spanish films, he said they gave him a headache. I voted during the entire decade of the nineties in Argentina, and always for candidates who didn't win. I worked in a secondhand bookstore every Saturday morning from the ages of twelve to fourteen. My mother's mother died when she was a girl, I don't know of what, and from then until she was a teenager, my mother and her sister lived in an orphanage; I think the only things my mother remembers about those years is that once she saw a nun without her habit on and that her sister stole her food. I was a fanatical Catholic between the ages of could and later I'd be empty and have nothing more to say, and that I was going to publish with the houses where I wanted to publish, and that I was going to meet loyal friends who would know how to drink and laugh, and that I was going to have the time to read everything I wanted to read, but also the resignation to accept that I wasn't going to be able to read it all, as always happens, and, in general, that things weren't going to go wrong. And in that moment, as I walked though the city without being observed by anyone except myself, I understood for the first time that the voice that had so often sounded in my head, especially in the worst of times, in the moments of greatest doubt, was an unknown voice while at the same time familiar because it was my own voice, or the voice of someone I was going to be, and that one day, after having seen it all and after having done everything and having returned, it would whisper to me, while I tried on a sweater in a store or read in a library or prepared an early dinner, that everything was going to be fine, and would promise me more books and more friends and more trips. Except then I wondered what would happen when I went back to the German city where I'd been living, if I would hear that voice again promising that there were going to be other days and I was going to see them all, and perhaps my father too, and that I was going to leave evidence of them, and I wondered if that voice would tell the truth this time or if it would tell a compassionate lie, as it had done so many times in the past.

52

A line of light came in through the lowered blind of my father's study; when the blind was lifted, however, the light seemed weaker to me than the line had indicated. I opened the curtains and turned on a table lamp, but even then the light was insufficient. My father used to tell my brother as a boy that he should go out and play and come back when he could no longer see his hands, but my brother could still see his hands at night. In that moment, though it wasn't yet night, I was the one who couldn't see mine. I felt a presence behind me and for a second I thought it was my father, coming to scold me for sneaking into his study, but then I saw that it was my brother. I think I'm going crazy, I said to him, I can't see my hands. My brother stared at me and said, It looks that way to me too. I didn't know if he was talking about my having gone crazy or that he couldn't see his hands; either way, a moment later he came back with a desk lamp that he put on the table and turned on along with the others. The light was still dim, but now I could make out some objects in the penumbra: a blade for cutting paper; a ruler; a jar of pencils, pens and

47

highlighters; and a typewriter standing on end to save space. On the desk there was a pile of folders, but I didn't touch them. I sat in my father's chair and looked at the garden, wondering how many hours he'd spent there and if he'd ever thought of me during that time. The study was freezing. I leaned forward and grabbed a folder from the pile. The folder was filled with information for a trip my father hadn't taken and perhaps now never would. I put it to one side and grabbed another that contained recent press clippings with his byline; I read the clippings for a while and then left them to one side. On a loose sheet of paper I found a list of books my father had recently bought: there was a title by Alexis de Tocqueville, another by Domingo Faustino Sarmiento, an atlas of Argentina's highways, a book about that music from the northeastern part of the country called chamamé and a book I'd written some time ago. In the next folder was a reproduction of an old photograph, enlarged to the point that it dissolved into dots. In it appeared my father, although, of course, he wasn't exactly my father, but rather whoever he had been before I met him: his hair was moderately long and he had sideburns and was holding a guitar; beside him there was a young woman with long, straight hair and an expression of surprising seriousness, a gaze that seemed to say she wasn't going to waste time because she had more important things to do than stay still for a photograph, she had to fight and die young. And I thought: I know that face, but later, reading the materials my father had gathered in that folder, I thought that I hadn't ever known it, that I'd never seen it and that I would have pre-ferred to continue that way, without knowing any-thing about the person behind that face, and also without knowing anything about my father's last weeks. You don't ever want to know certain things, because what you know belongs to you, and there are certain things you never want to own.

II

He would have to think of an attitude, or a style that would turn what was written into a document.

—César Aira, *The Three Dates*

1

The folder was thirty by twenty-two centimeters, made of a very lightweight cardboard in a pale yellow color. It was two centimeters thick and enclosed by two elastic bands that could have once been white but at this point had a slightly brown tone; one of the bands held the folder from top to bottom and the other along its width, which made them form a cross; more specifically, a Latin cross. Near the lower edge of the folder there was a sticker carefully positioned on the yellow cardboard. The letters were black, printed on a gray background; just one word and that word was a name: *Burdisso.*

2

Inside the folder was another sticker, which included the full name of a person, Alberto José Burdisso.

3

On the next page was a photograph of a man who looked withdrawn, who had barely distinguishable features. It accompanied an article titled "The Mysterious Case of a Missing Resident." The text of the article is as follows:

Alberto Burdisso is a citizen of El Trébol and has been an employee at the Club Trebolense for many years. The mystery as regarding his person began to grow when on Monday he did not present his person [sic] at work and neither did he do so on Tuesday. From that moment began an elaborate investigation. His coworkers at the institution first investigated by their own means, going to his home on Calle Corrientes and seeing that there was no movement inside, ongly [sic] his bicycle left in the courtyard, watched over by his dog, who was outside.

No one has seen "Burdi" since Sunday, and he would have mentioned to one of his coworkers if he was going to the city of *osario for the weekend. He would have received his salary between Friday and Saturday, since the Club Trebolense pays its employees on the last workday of the month.

"They called us on Monday at 10 p.m. on

the 101 emergency line," declared Captain Hugo Iussa to *El Trébol Digital*. "A coworker told us that he hadn't shown up for work at the Club Trebolense. We interviewed neighbors, and we notified the Court of First Instance in San Jorge, which authorized us to make a 'file of inquiry of whereabouts,' but for now, at this point, that doesn't mean that we've ruled out another possibility"[?]. He also added: "We reviewed his domicile and we did not perceive any signs of violence. We have several hypotheses and we are hoping to find him."

Coworkers last saw Burdisso on Saturday as he left work at lunchtime lunchtime [*sic*]. There, to a doorman of the Institution he mentioned the possibility of going to *osario for a stroll.

According to neighbors, Alberto José Burdisso, 60 years old, was last seen in the vicinity of his own neighborhood, on Calle Corrientes at number 438 on Sunday afternoon.

Another peculiarity of the resident is that he has no relatives in the city, he only had a disappeared sister during the period of the Military Dictatorship and some cousins in the rural area of El Trébol but with whom he barely had any contact.

Source: *El Trébol Digital,* June 4, 2008

4

This article, with its absurd syntax, was followed by an enlargement of the image that accompanied it in the digital edition. The photograph showed a man with a round face, small eyes and a mouth with thick lips locked in a strange smile. The man wore his hair very short—it was either light or gray—and in the photograph he was being given a commemorative plate of some kind by someone only partially in the frame. The man—all signs point to the fact that it was Alberto Burdisso himself—wore a pale V-necked cotton sports shirt from which hung some rimless eyeglasses the man, perhaps out of vanity, had taken off before being photographed. The text of the commemorative plate was illegible in the photograph.

5

Then it must be because he lived in the same small town where my father grew up, the town to which he periodically returned and where my sister lives, I thought the first time I read the news article. Now I also think that behind the abstruse syntax and the ridiculous police jargon—how else to describe sentences such as "but for now, at this point, that doesn't mean that we've ruled out another possibility"?—there was a symmetry, according to which I was searching for my father and my father was giving his account of a search for someone else, someone he may have known and who had disappeared.

6

There is also the mystery of who was giving his account and who had taken an interest in the search, but that mystery is almost impossible for me to solve.

7

What did I remember about El Trébol? An expanse of field, sometimes yellow and sometimes green but always right next to the houses and the streets, as if in my memories the town is much smaller than the statistics indicate. A little forest of trees beside some abandoned, overgrown train tracks: in the forest there were frogs and iguanas, which rested on the tracks during the hottest hours of the day and fled if they noticed you were stalking them. The neighborhood kids used to say that if you found yourself confronted by an iguana, you should always be sure to keep in front of it, since if the iguana lashed at you with its tail it could cut off your leg. This game was also popular: We used to capture frogs in an irrigation ditch and stick them, still alive, in a plastic bag, which we then placed in the street as a car was passing. The game was, after the car had destroyed the bag, each of us would try to put together an entire frog with the pieces scattered on the sidewalk; whoever finished a frog first won. On the street where we used to play this frog puzzle game, there was an old bar and warehouse that had been swallowed up by the city, and my paternal grandfather used to go there at dusk to drink a glass of wine and sometimes play cards. In the summer you could get ice cream at a store called Blanrec, whose owner, I think, was actually called Lino; I used to read a lot when we spent summers in El Trébol, and take long naps and, in general, spend a lot of time walking the streets, which were like the streets in the small American Midwestern towns from 1950s movies; most of the buildings were homes, and they were all always closed up, with the blinds slightly open to enable people to spy on what was happening outside. At dusk the spying came out into the open, as if a ban prohibiting it only at certain hours had been lifted, and people used to bring chairs out onto the sidewalk and sit and chat with the neighbors. Sometimes you also saw people on horseback. Naturally, everyone knew each other and they said good morning or good afternoon or whatever it was, greeting each other with first names or nicknames because each one of those names came with a story that was the story of the individual who bore it and of his entire family, past and present. Some of my father's uncles were deaf-mutes and, therefore, I was the kid from the deaf family or the grandson of the painter; the deaf-mutes made floor mosaics, a profession I think they learned in jail, and they had dogs that responded to names they could say in spite of not being able to really speak: Cof and Pop. There were never thefts of any importance in town and people usually left their doors open in the summer and their cars unlocked and their bicycles tossed on their front lawns. Around the back of my grandparents' house, a man had some land where he raised rabbits. Another had a grocery store with shelves that reached the ceiling; he was very tall. I liked the bread that man sold. I also liked the iced tea my grandmother made and the songs my grandfather whistled. He was always whistling or humming; his hands were destroyed by the turpentine he used to remove paint stains but, from what I understood, he'd been through worse. There wasn't a real bookstore or a library

8

The next article was from the same digital newspaper, published a day after the first. It read:

Alberto Burdisso has not turned up. 72 hours have passed since his disappearance, there are not many clues to guide those searching for him in the city and in the region. After an intense day on Wednesday in which the local police relentlessly took declarations from coworkers, family members, neighbors, and friends, the Volunteer Firemen, along with the police themselves, scoured the region, rural roads, farmhouses, ruined and abandoned houses that border and are next to the neighborhood where Burdisso has his abode, with a totally negative result. "We carried out patrols and searches in suburban and urban areas in spiral but to date we've found nothing. We'll continue all day today with more searching. We worked the canals, sewers and even wastelands, but, for the moment, nothing," explained Hugo Yussa to "ElTrebolDigital" [sic]. Alberto Burdisso was last seen on Sunday night near his domicile, on Calle Corrientes number 400.

On Wednesday evening during the evening hours, another important detail emerged:

Burdisso's debit card was swallowed by the ATM of Banco Nación. "The card thing happened on Saturday," explained Iussa, of the 9th Precinct. The search operation asked the banks Credicoop (from thence the card was issued) and Banco Nación (in who's [sic] machine it was found) to offer information on the financial movements in the accounts of the missing resident.

9

The following pages were stapled together in the upper left corner; they were printouts, shoddy ones, of a short history of El Trébol that my father had corrected and annotated by hand:

The birth of El Trébol [illegible]. There was no single act or explicit desire [crossed out]. The situation is even further complicated by the almost simultaneous design of three towns: [. . .] Pueblo Passo in 1889, El Trébol in 1890 and Tais in 1892. The conjunction of these three towns came about in 1894 when, by provincial decree, the Municipality was established, all under the single denomination of El Trébol, whose [illegible].

On the 15th of January 1890 the first train left Cañada de Gómez [illegible] immigrant family members and friends with the intention of establishing themselves in those lands [illegible] of the Central Argentine Railway like the founding date of El Trébol, [crossed out] their complex interrelation [illegible] rural [illegible].

The name emerged during the construction of the branch line of the Central Argentine Railway [illegible] financed with capital from Britain, since this subsidiary company was responsible for naming the stations that [illegible] three stations in a row were named with symbols of Great Britain. "Las Rosas" for the red and white roses in the English coat of arms; "Los Cardos"—Thistles—in honor of Scotland; and "El Trébol"—Clover—for the flower typical of Ireland [illegible] first colonists that came to settle around 1889 were [illegible] in 1895 the national census of that year calculated 3,333 rural settlers and 333 in the urban area, which is [illegible] mostly Italians, although there were also Spaniards, Frenchmen, Germans, Swiss, Yugoslavians, Russians, "Turks" who arrived crowded into boats with third-class tickets and for the most part [illegible].

In 1914 Mr. Victorio De Lorenzi and Mr. Marcos de la Torre bought the land where [illegible] and in 1918 some expansions were undertaken, the police station and an [illegible] assembly hall was built. In 1941 when the fiftieth anniversary of El Trébol was celebrated they [illegible] the resolution to erect a monument. The sculptress Elisa Damiano [illegible] was entrusted with the creation of said monument. The sculpture was designed atop a base of four figures with intertwined hands symbolizing the human prototypes of our region. It was crowned by a figure of a woman symbolizing the abundance of the harvest, depicted by a sheaf of wheat and a bag of grain. The plaque placed on the western face has this inscription: "The town of El Trébol to its first immigrants."

In 1901 a small group of Spaniards established the Spanish Society, in 1905 [illegible] the exclusive work of the members since they built it themselves, working on Sundays and thus managed to open the Teatro Cervantes. Between 1929 and 1930 the theater, interior furnishings and dressing rooms were expanded. The main holiday was the Spanish Processions, celebrated on the 12th of October, Día de la Raza. Grand dances were organized and the hall was lit with gas lanterns because there was no electricity. There were hired bands and bagpipers. The musicians came from Buenos Aires, and the townspeople waited for them at the train station, marching from there through the streets, handing out lit torches to those accompanying the bands [illegible] collapses in 1945 [illegible].

In 1949 it was resolved to erect a Flagpole and an Altar to the Nation in the center of the plaza, for which the traditional [illegible] was demolished. In addition the plaza was given the name of General San Martín [illegible] inaugurate the first Catholic church in El Trébol, dedicated to Saint Lawrence the Martyr. In 1921 the Priest Joaquín García de la Vega was [illegible] and in 1925 was placed [illegible] monumental building in Tuscan Renaissance style [crossed out].

In September [added in pencil: "1894"] Enrique Miles, Santiago Rossini and José Tais were appointed to build the cemetery. On November 19th of that same year the Italian Mutual Benefit Society "Italian Star" was officially established. In the year 1896 the first gravedigger was named, Casimiro Vega [illegible]. In the year 1897 they decided to build the municipal abattoir [illegible]. On the 16th of September 1946 the Athletic Club was founded. The [illegible] inaugurated the Volunteer Blood Donors Club.

In the year 1984 the necessary steps were taken to raise the town to the status of city through sanction of a provincial law [illegible].

National Day of the Milking Machine [illegible] construction of the first mechanical milking machine in South America [illegible] the National Queen, selected from representatives of the Santa Fe geographical province.

The first party was organized by the Club Atlético Trebolense, in [illegible] of the Tango: due to the notable boost that the city's music experienced in El Trébol during the last [illegible] that played for its native sons [crossed out] in the month of February in the brand-new permanent parade grounds, organized by the Town Hall of El Trébol, where one can enjoy the procession of floats, bands, Carnival Queen contestants, a foam machine and the popular dance [illegible] in the heart of what is called the "Humid Pampa," the most important cereal growing region in South America and one of the most important in the world in terms of the quality and quantity of arable land, suitable for all types of vegetable species and livestock rearing.

10

Another article, from the same paper as the others and published on June 6, 2008:

Commissioner Odel Bauducco gave details to "ElTrebolDigital" [sic] about the intense search that is being realized. "From a personal and professional standpoint, I began to work on the search for this person. The Firemen offered to work and they are working beside us combing the area. For example, yesterday the Fire Department worked in the rural area, in María Susana, Bandurrias and Los Cardos, without results." On the crossing of borders in the search to find him, Bauducco noted: "On that very Sunday, a photo of this person arrived in every police station in the country. We can trace his movements up to six on Sunday evening, when this person went to a private residence. After that nobody has been able to tell me anything more. I can't comment on what he did or what was said in that residence because the matter is sub judice."

The Commissioner also rejected some rumors that have traveled the streets in the last few hours: "I am not aware that someone saw him on Monday morning at a bank. The debit card was found before he was last seen. I even have in my possession the ticket print-out receipt of the card that was found in his domicile. Now we are asking people who know something about him to come forward with information."

11

On a printed page, there is a series of facts that seem to have been taken from an encyclopedia—"32°11'21"S 61°43'34"O; 92 meters above sea level; 344 km?; 10,506 inhabitants, approximately; term used to refer to the inhabitants: trebolense; postal code: S2535; telephone prefix: 03401"—and below that are some handwritten notes, probably made by my father: "two soccer teams: the Club Atlético Trebolense and the Club Atlético El Expreso; 'Sky Blue' and 'The Green Bug'; and the 'Club San Lorenzo,' which is next to the church; four primary schools and two secondary schools and one special needs school; 16,000 inhabitants."

12

No news on the Burdisso case. Alberto José Burdisso hasn't shown up. The earth must have swallowed him up last Sunday. A week now since his disappearance, the information and clues are skimpy. Only his debit card has appeared, stuck in the ATM of the

Banco Nación on Saturday. After that nothing more is known. The fliers distributed by his coworkers indicate their desperation and interest in finding leads. The police have said nothing or very little and the rest is sub judice. The Volunteer Firemen finished their search of the entire region last Thursday. The rumor that the body of the missing employee of the Club Trebolense was found lifeless in a well was quickly denied. They past [sic] declarations to the police and, in addition, conducted searches of different places. We, the citizens of El Trébol, demand an explanation or a response to a mystery that we cannot ignore, because this could happen to all of us.

El Trébol Digital, June 9, 2008

13

A flier, its upper left corner wrinkled, carries the same photograph of the missing man that accompanied the article on June 4, and the text

ALBERTO JOSÉ BURDISSO.
WHEREABOUTS UNKNOWN.
LAST SEEN ON JUNE 1, 2008.
COMMUNICATE ANY INFORMATIONS [SIC]
TO HIS COWORKERS AT C. A. TREBOLENSE,

POLICE 101, FIREMEN 100
ANY INFORMATION APPRECIATED,
COWORKERS.

14

A survey, published in the same local paper under the title "What Do You Think About the Burdisso Case?," reveals the main theories about the disappearance and the reactions of the town's inhabitants. The results are the following:

He's going to show up (2.38%); He's never going to be seen again (13.10%); He's going to be found alive (3.57%); He's going to be found dead (25.00%); He moved without telling anyone (4.76%); This was a crime of passion (25.00%); He was kidnapped (8.33%); He is dead by natural causes (3.57%); He left town for some reason (2.38%); I don't know what to think (11.90%).

A quick glance at these figures reveals that most of the town's inhabitants—many of them involved in the search for the missing man, as the local press states—believed at the time that he was going to be found alive, and that the root of his disappearance was a crime of passion. But who would commit a crime of passion against a common worker in a provincial club, some sort of Faulknerian simple-ton whose presence had gone unnoticed by every-one except a small circle, who was tolerated the same way a dust storm or a mountain is tolerated, with indifferent resignation?

15

By the way, if the aforementioned percentages are added up the result is 99.99 percent. The remain-ing 0.01, which is missing or simply represents an error in the survey, seems to occupy the place of the disappeared man: he is there as that which can-not be said, that which cannot even be named. The writers of the survey left out some possible explanations for the disappearance that we can briefly mention here, even though they're admit-tedly improbable—he won the lottery, he is in France or Australia, he was abducted by aliens, et cetera—which prove that not even reality can be absolutely reduced to a statistic.

16

Ten days without Burdisso: Alberto José Burdisso lived alone in his house on Calle Corrientes, number 400 of the city of El Trébol. His domicile is some four blocks from the Club Trebolense, where [sic] he frequented mornings and afternoons from Monday to Saturday for many years to carry out his work tasks. He was a simple, popular character and friendly with those around him. He barely had any family, except for some relative who lives in the rural area of the city with whom he had no relationship. [. . .] On Monday June 2nd, when he didn't show up for work, his coworkers at the Club missed him and that afternoon they called the police and mentioned his absence. That very evening, when his friends went to his house, they found his bicycle left on the patio and beside it, his loyal dog, who followed him wherever he went. [. . .] The city's firemen completed spiral searches from his domicile outward. Every rural road, every abandoned, dilapidated house and uninabited [sic] home as well as the sewer and irrigation ditches. There were four or five days of desperate searching. They went as far as Las Bandurrias, Bouquet, Pueblo Casas, María Susana and Los Cardos. [. . .] Meanwhile, 10 days have now passed since his disappearance. Associated but not minor facts: it could be noted that "Burdi" came into some money three years ago [. . .] of which he had nothing left; he lived off a salary that the club religiously paid him on the last working day of each month (coincidencelly [*sic*] he was paid the Friday before he disappeared); he was a person who kept "temporary company" and not much more.

Nobody knows anything. Nobody saw anything, nobody heard anything. In the city everybody whispers about it, as if they were afraid of something, without knowing what. If they let things like this happen, tomorrow the same thing could happen to any of us.

Commissioner Bauducco declared: "I don't feel pressure from local residents because these things happen and we are working hard to try to resolve [the case]. [. . .] We have new witness statements and new leads to follow. There may or may not be news in the coming hours. [. . .] I invite people to come forward with any information that they will be welcome [*sic*]. There have been no arrests because there is no crime, in principle. It is clear that, in the case of the person arriving deceased, it would no longer be a missing person's case and we would work on other theories."

Later Bauducco said: "In the Burdisso home no signs of violence were found, nor any signs that he was planning a trip. The

door was closed and there are other teensy
details."

El Trébol Digital, June 11, 2008

17

In this article, for the first time it becomes clear
that the Burdisso case has been transformed from a
police matter—pathetic, yes, confused, yes, but also
pretty juvenile—into some sort of vague threat that
affects society at large. "Nobody knows anything.
Nobody saw anything, nobody heard anything. In
the city everybody whispers about it, as if they
were afraid of something," writes the article's anonymous author. And yet the author never speci-
fies what this fear is, if it's the disappearance or
whatever is behind it, an accident or a murder,
perhaps related to the money, although supposedly
there wasn't any left. And why did a Faulknerian
idiot receive all that money? I wondered. And what
were those "teensy details" mentioned by the police
officer? At this point the missing man himself
ceased to be a cause for concern among the town's
inhabitants and, in his place, what emerged was
a collective fear, the fear of a recurrence and the
fear of losing the almost proverbial tranquillity of
El Trébol. At this point, to put it another way, the
inevitable shift occurred from individual victim to

collective victim, as witnessed by the following article, published on June 12 in the same local newspaper as the previous ones:

> The friends of Alberto Burdisso, the citizen mysteriously disappeared 11 days ago, organized a march to the Plaza San Martín to call for the resolution of the case that is, at this point in the days [sic], a complete mystery to all Trebolenses. The rally is set for five in the afternoon and a large gathering is expected. On Wednesday morning, Mabel Burga pointed out on Radio El Trébol: "Those who feel it's important to stand up for Alberto and for safety in El Trébol should go."

18

Then, in my father's folder, there was a map folded in four; it was a map of the region of El Trébol, marked with a yellow highlighter and two pens, one with red ink and the other blue. Entire areas had been highlighted. The blue pen followed the itinerary of the policemen in charge of the investigation. The red pen marked the search itinerary of someone else, who had mainly opted for places where the police hadn't looked, thickets on the outskirts of town and a nearby brook. There were some illegible notes written in a cramped, hasty hand on the edges of the map. That handwriting— I can still recognize it—was my father's. The map was crumpled and had traces of mud on the upper right corner, which made me think that my father had used it out in the field, during a search.

19

A headline on June 13, from *El Trébol Digital:* "Now They Search for Burdisso with Dogs."

20

That same day, the regional press showed inter- est in the case for the first time; in my father's file there was a photocopy of an article published in the newspaper *La Capital de *osario* with the title "El Trébol Marches for the Recovery of Local Man." Someone, I suppose my father, had under- lined the main thrust of the article, which is the following:

> "No to impunity and yes to life" is the slo- gan of this march that will demand that the disappearance investigation be carried to its

final conclusion. [. . .] In his home, police personnel found the lights on, with signs of a struggle and some belongings apparently missing. [. . .] On Tuesday one of the city's banking institutions brought the local police Burdisso's debit card, which had been held by an ATM, although there was no video footage that would help identify who had tried to use it. In addition, it has emerged that the card was retained by the ATM on Saturday May 31 around midday; which is to say, 24 hours before his disappearance. [. . .] It is known that the money didn't last long and that with part of it he bought a house with one of the women whose company he kept. He also bought cars and it has been stated that, after receiving this sum, he was linked with "loose living" people, leading him to squander it [. . .].

21

A naïve reader might wonder why the regional press states that the police found signs of violence in the missing man's home when the local press maintains that this wasn't the case, that when his friends went looking for him they found the front door locked and the bicycle—not to mention the oh-so-literary detail of the "loyal dog" who followed his master "wherever he went"—in front of the house. The reader might wonder why the security camera at the cash machine wasn't working at the moment the missing man's debit card was used for the last time. Once again the naïve reader might wonder who the "loose living" people the article referred to were, but there, for someone who has lived in the city where the events took place, the answer is simple: a "loose living" person is, in El Trébol, anyone who wasn't born in the city. A foreigner. Even if this foreignness is based only on a couple of kilometers' distance, or the supposed misfortune of having been born on the other side of a gully or beyond a copse of eucalyptus trees or on the other side of the train tracks, anywhere on the whole planet that extends past the city and that, for the inhabitants of El Trébol, is an inhospitable, hostile world where the cold cuts your flesh and the heat burns and there is no shade or shelter.

22

At that point, the articles my father had collected began to run together. The reader retains barely a few sentences: "The firemen searched for Burdisso in rural regions"; "[. . .] with negative results [. . .]"; "'It is very difficult to search like this, without any leads,' stated the Fire Chief, Raúl Dominio, to [. . .]"; "Last Friday the search was resumed by police staff, fireman and municipal employees, [. . .] this time a larger amount of personnel was used and they scoured each sector inch by inch"; "the Special Dog Brigade of the Santa Fe Police and specialized detectives worked on his search, but they weren't able to find the man," et cetera. Of all the articles, one stood out, published in *El Ciudadano & La Región* of the city of *osario. One of its paragraphs began by saying: "Alberto José Burdisso lives alone in his house at 400 Calle Corrientes in the city of El Trébol"; I knew this was the newspaper where my father worked and I also knew there was a wish or a hope in that sentence, found in the verb tense, and I understood the writer was my father and, had he been able to dispense with journalistic conventions, he would have been more direct and expressed his conviction, his wish or his hope without relying on any rhetoric, laying bare without any euphemisms: "Alberto José Burdisso lives."

23

In a multitudinous gathering of almost 1000 people, the city of El Trébol complained about the lack of justice in the Burdisso case and the lack of resolution in his mysterious disappearance.

From five in the afternoon on a holiday

Monday, the Plaza began to fill with people who, gathering of their own volition, signed a list of demands that will be set [sic] to the hands of Judge Eladio García of the city of San Jorge. [. . .] First at the event was Dr. Roberto Maurino, a childhood schoolmate of Burdisso's, who spoke to the audience. [. . .], Maurino stated to an attentive crowd that was continually signing petitions. Shortly afterward came Gabriel Piumetti, one of the organizers of the march, along with his mother, who pointed out [. . .] The people applauded every word and shouts of "Justice, justice!!!" were heard in the amphitheater for a long time.

After the first speeches, someone in the public shout [sic], "Let the police commissioner speak!," as he was among the people. It was then that the chief of the city's Fourth Precinct, Oriel Bauducco, expressed [. . .]. At that moment irate demands from the public arose and various questions were heard: "Why did they search for Burdisso with dogs ten days after his disappearance?" fired off one woman, and another question immediately followed: "Wide [sic] you clear out Burdisso's house two days after his disappearance when it should have been taped off?" That was the moment of highest tension in the Plaza, the crowd staring insistently at the superior officer, waiting for a reply that never came. [. . .] struggled to say Bauducco, who after listening how various residents complained [sic] the lack of road blocks in the streets and the absence of patrolling in the city.

Minutes later Mayor Fernando Almada addressed the crowd saying [. . .]. In addition to Almada, among those gathered were the city councilmen, the former mayor, now secretary of [. . .], and the employees and Executive Board of the Club Trebolense, where Alberto Burdisso worked.

El Trébol Digital, June 17, 2008

24

In the lower corner of the article was a photograph. It showed a group of people—perhaps there really were a thousand, as the anonymous writer of the article claims, though it doesn't look like it—listening to a bald speaker. In the background of the photograph was a church I recognized, with a disproportionately tall tower, which looked like a swan curled up on the shore, stretching out its neck in an attempt to find nourishment. Seeing it, I remembered my father once told me that my paternal great-grandfather had climbed up the old tower, which had been damaged in an earthquake or some other natural disaster, in order to clear out the rubble so it could be rebuilt, but because the tower's wooden beams were rotted from exposure to the elements, my great-grandfather was risking his life, not to mention the inevitable thread of paternities that led to us; but in that moment I couldn't remember if my father had told me the story or if it was made up, a flight of fancy based on the similarity between the thinness of the tower and that of my paternal grandfather as I remembered him, and still today I don't know if it was my paternal great-grandfather or my maternal great-grandfather who climbed the tower, nor do I know if at any point the church tower suffered damage, since there aren't many earthquakes or natural disasters in El Trébol.

25

"Three cases of homicide, disappearance and kidnapping in one year in the city," affirmed another article, pointing out: "Three unresolved cases."

26

Once more, the key word here was *disappearance*, repeated in one way or another in all the articles, like a black armband worn by every cripple and have-not in Argentina.

26

An article in the morning paper *La Capital* of the city of *osario on June 18 expanded, corrected and contextualized the previous article: the demonstration had brought together eight hundred people, not a thousand, and the list of demands requested "that justice be done," which, in addition to the way most of the speeches alternated between the present and past tenses, made it seem as if the demonstrators suspected Burdisso had been murdered and they wanted the authorities to consider this possibility. At the same time, the growing demands, with their explicit warning that what had happened to Burdisso could also happen to others, seemed to shift the focus from an isolated police event to a generalized, omnipresent threat. It could be said that the eight hundred people who took part in the demonstration—an insignificant segment of the population, if, as another article maintains, the city has thirteen thousand inhabitants—were already beginning to switch from demanding "justice" for Burdisso to demanding it for themselves and their families. No one wanted to suffer Burdisso's fate, but no one at that point knew what had happened to him and no one wondered why he had been chosen instead of someone else, someone else among those who exorcized their fears with a demonstration and a list of demands.

27

A couple of letters to the editor were published in *El Trébol Digital* on June 18 and 19 of that year: one denounced "the black humor" of an anonymous text message that proposed marching for the disappearance not of Burdisso but of a rival sports team; the other wondered if Burdisso had been "swallowed up by the earth."

28

A survey, published on the same site on June 18, contained hardly any variation from the one published a week earlier.

> He's going to show up (2.64% as opposed to the previous 2.38%); He's never going to be seen again (11.45% as opposed to 13.10%); He's going to be found alive (2.64% as opposed to 3.57%); He's going to be found

dead (28.63% as opposed to 25.00%); He
moved without telling anyone (5.29% as
opposed to 4.76%); This was a crime of passion (24.67% as opposed to 25.00%); He was
kidnapped (5.29% as opposed to 8.33%); He
is dead by natural causes (2.20% as opposed
to 3.57%); He left town for some reason
(5.73% as opposed to 2.38%); I don't know
what to think (11.45% as opposed to 11.90%).

29

The title of another article: "Agents from Crimi-
nalistics Arrive in the City for the Burdisso Case."
The date of its publication: June 19, 2008. The
defense of the actions taken by the local police,
from the chief of the Eighteenth Regional Unit:

[. . .] on the speed with which Burdisso's
dwelling was occupied and the delay in the
arrival of the Brigade of dogs to the city, Dr.
Gómez pointed out: "They are two separate
issues. As in regards therein to the dwelling it must be understood that as there is
no proof of any tragic events the dwelling cannot be kept unoccupied, and the
issue of the dogs is because they were looking for finer elements [sic]. The dogs were
sent in and will be sent in again soon. We
are searching for Burdisso throughout the

country, as we have been from the very first moment." [...]

A declaration, from the same civil servant: "For the moment we are searching to find him alive."

30

I want him to show up if he went off on his own, and if he's found dead, I want the guilty parties to be found. I'm asking everyone who was there [at the demonstration on the seventeenth], [who] also did it out of obligation, nobody is exempt, it could happen to any of us.

Raquel P. Sopranzi in
El Trébol Digital on June 20, 2008

31

As I continue reading my father's file, I come across a headline from *El Trébol Digital* on June 20, stamped on an idyllic image of the town with the incongruence of a modern device in an old photograph: "Now They Discover a Body in an Abandoned Well."

32

This morning, at approximately 10:30, the excavation unit of the Volunteer Firemen of El Trébol, following intense search, founds [sic] a body at the depths of an abandoned well in a field 8 kilometers from the city of El Trébol, where there is an old abandoned building with two old water wells. The body appeared beneath much rubble and corrugated metal sheets. The police worked at the site while the firemen operated on the outside of the cavity. At approximately twelve thirty, they managed to extract a male body of some eighty-five or ninety kilos and approximately 1.70 in height tressed [sic] in pants and blue cardigan and white T-shirt. The judge of the city of San Jorge, Dr. Eladio García, along with special units and staff from the 18th Regional Unit based in Sastre, arrived on the scene.

Dr. Pablo Cándiz, forensic doctor, made the first inspection of the cadaver, which was later transferred to the city of Santa Fe to be autopsied.

"We have no information on other missing person cases in the region," stated the Deputy Chief of the 18th Regional Unit, Commissioner Agustín Hiedro, to "ElTrebolDigital" [sic] from the site[,] and added:

"We found the site based on a report from someone who had been in that field and noticed a penetrating odor surrounding a well. We works [*sic*] intensely in the late noon on Thursday until due to low light it was decided that we would continue our work on Friday morning, and so we came out here first thing."

The body found in the depths of the crevice has physical similar [*sic*] characteristics to Alberto Burdisso, who mysteriously disappeared exactly twenty days ago.

33

Some photographs accompanied the article. In the first you could see some five people looking into a well; since all the figures were leaning over, you couldn't make out their faces, though you could see that one of them, the third from the left, situated precisely in the middle, had white hair and wore glasses. In the next photograph you could see a fireman descending into the well on a rope; the fireman wore a white helmet with the number thirty on it. In another photograph you could see the fireman already inside the well, barely illuminated by the light from the mouth of the hole and a flashlight attached to his helmet. In the next one you could see three firemen with their gear; in the background, a coffin or box wrapped in black plastic. In the two photographs that followed, you could see five people carrying the coffin; one of them covered his face with a handkerchief, maybe to avoid the smell of the cadaver. In the next photograph you could see the firemen putting the coffin into a van that perhaps served as an ambulance and perhaps not; there was a man filming, with one hand in his pocket; two other men smiling. In the final photograph, which broke the apparent chronological continuity, you could see the coffin before it got taken to the van; it was on the ground, which was broken into big dark mounds of clumpy earth, and you couldn't see anyone near it; the coffin was completely alone.

34

Question: "Is it true that the body has a scar on the torso like the one Burdisso had?"

Answer: "It is true that the body has a scar like this."

Question: "What information will the autopsy reveal?"

Answer: "The autopsy will determine the causal [sic] of death and the reasons for the state of putrefaction."

Question: "In what state was the body?"

Answer: "The body has a series of circumstances that the doctors will mention in their report."

Question: "What does that mean? Injuries?"

Answer: "Exactly. The doctors confirmed that."

Question: "On the face or on the body?"

Answer: "On the body."

Question: "Bullet wounds?"

Answer: "At this point it does not appear so."

Question: "Blunt force trauma?"

Answer: "There are no details of that kind [. . .]."

Question: "Has anyone been arrested?"

Answer: "There are people of interest in El Trébol and in other areas."

Question: "Could this change the determination of the cause of death?"

Answer: "That will be decided by a judge [. . .]."

Question: "Are there fugitives from justice?"

Answer: "The people summoned have appeared."

Question: "Who notified the authorities about the body? Is it true that it was a hunter?"

Answer: "The person who revealed knowledge could be someone who hunts, who smelled the odors."

Conversation between the writer and Jorge Gómez, of the Eighteenth Regional Unit, *El Trébol Digital,* June 20, 2008. Title of the article: "We Have Information That the Body Found Could Be Alberto Burdisso's"

35

We came on Thursday night with police personnel. All indications were that we would find something. It's an unpleasant place still during the day, very dangerous, and it was impossible to continue after dark. So we returned with eighteen men and we worked at a depth of ten meters with tripod and rigs making it easier to extract the body. [. . .] It's not the first time we've done this. [. . .] They [volunteer firemen Javier Bergamasco and "Melli" Maciel] had to do the hardest part, but it was a team effort.

Declarations of the head of the Volunteer Firemen Corps of El Trébol, Raúl Dominio, to *El Trébol Digital,* June 20, 2008

36

Even before the results of the autopsy on the cadaver were made public, the accumulated facts—particularly the scar mentioned in the conversation between the chief of the Eighteenth Regional Police Unit and an anonymous journalist—and an explicit desire for the missing man to be found (dead or alive, really) seemed to have led to the immediate unspoken conclusion that the cadaver was Burdisso; in fact, the following article collected by my father, an article from the twenty-first, stated outright that "the body of Alberto Burdisso will arrive in the city at approximately one thirty" and gave the name of the funeral home where the body would be laid out, the prayers said at the parish of Saint Lawrence the Martyr—the church in the background of the photograph of the demonstration four days earlier—and a funeral procession through streets with names like San Lorenzo, Entre Ríos, Candiotti and Córdoba. However, the identity of the body found in the well should not be accepted by the reader before asking why someone would want to murder a Faulknerian idiot, an adult with the mind of a child, someone who didn't drink, didn't gamble and had no money, someone who had to work every day to survive, doing the most menial of tasks like cleaning a swimming pool or repairing a roof. That question, which ran through the next few articles in my father's file, is perhaps a public one. A private question—so intimate that I could ask it only of myself, and at that point I didn't know the answer—was why my father had taken such an interest in the disappearance of someone he may not have even known, one of those faces seen in passing, associated with a name or two but of no great significance, part of the landscape, like a mountain or a river. So it was actually a double mystery: not only the particular circumstances of Burdisso's death but also the motives that led my father to search for him, as if that search would solve a greater mystery more deeply obscured by reality.

37

More photographs: a white car stopped in front of a crowd, mostly of children, who were applauding at the doors of a building with a sign that read "Club Atlético Trebolense M. S. y B."; I didn't know what the initials meant, but the figure on the sign— a disproportionately muscular man, kneeling, holding up a C.A.T. emblem—was familiar; bunches of flowers emerged from the car's windows and seemed about to fall onto the asphalt. The next photograph showed the same scene from another angle, the photographer situated amid the mourners; his location allowed the viewer to see spectators gathered on the facing sidewalk. There were more photographs, taken in the same moment but from different angles; what most caught my eye was the contrast between the naked colossus who presided over the sign with the initials and the coats worn by the spectators. Then there were two images of an old man who stood speaking beside the car; the old man was bald, he wore glasses and a dark coat; one of the bunches of flowers coming out of the car's window had some sort of sash with a phrase, of which only the word *executive* could be read. The old man's face was familiar to me, and I wondered if he might be that dentist who had taken a fish bone out of my throat when I was a boy, a dentist whose hands shook and consequently instilled more fear in me as they handled the forceps than the fish bone itself had. Then there was a photograph that was easier for me to identify, even though the identification came quite fast and seemed to gush out, as if my memory, instead of evoking the recollection, regurgitated it. It was the entrance to the local cemetery and there were several dozen people forming a corridor in front of the car with the flowers; in the background of the image was a palm tree that seemed to shiver from the cold. In the next photograph, the crowd is seen from another angle showing a row of trees and a stretch of flat, empty land. Then there are two trite funeral photographs: one of some people walking with floral wreaths through the main entrance to the cemetery and toward the spot where the photographer must have stood, the figures breaking up into fragments if you look quickly—a mustached face, a hedge, two ties, a jacket, the surprised face of a child, a sweater over sweatpants, someone looking back; and one of four people holding up the coffin beside a niche dug into the wall—one man facing away and another man looking directly at the photographer with a slight expression of reproach. Then there was an image of a plaque that read: "R.I.P. Dora R. de Burdisso ✝ 8.21.1956 [or it could be 1958, the photograph wasn't in sharp focus] / Your husband and children with love"; it was probably the plaque that covered the niche before the coffin was deposited, probably referring to the dead man's grandmother or mother—but then, where is his father buried?—so perhaps it was a family crypt.

38

Then there was one last photograph of the event, and when I saw it I was surprised and confused, as if I had just seen a dead man approaching along a path with the infernal red setting sun silhouetted behind his back. It was my father just as I would see him in the hospital, in his final years: bald with a white beard on his thin face, very similar to his own father as I remembered him, with large rim-less glasses, the glasses of a policeman or a mafi-oso, with his hands in the pockets of a white coat, talking, his throat wrapped with a plaid scarf that I thought I had given him at some point as a gift. Beside him were other men, who contemplated him with sad faces, as if they knew my father was talking about a dead man without knowing that he would soon be one of them, that he was going to enter a dark, bottomless well that everyone who dies falls into, but my father didn't know it yet and they didn't want to tell him. There were eleven men standing behind my father, as if my father were the sacked coach of a soccer team that had just lost the championship; one wore a jacket and tie, but the rest wore leather coats and one, a long scarf that seemed about to strangle him. Some of them looked at the ground. I looked at my father and couldn't quite understand what he was doing there, talking in that cemetery on a cold afternoon, an afternoon in which the living and the dead should have taken refuge in the shelter of their homes or their tombs and in the resigned consolation of memory.

39

From the June 21, 2008, edition of *El Trébol Digital*:

Alberto José Burdisso lived aloan [*sic*] but left this world with a crowd. Because a multitude, crying out for justice, accompanied him en masse to his final resting place. Following the prayers for the dead in the parish of Saint Lawrence the Mar-

tyr, completely packed, a funeral procession several blocks long changed its route to
pass by the Club Trebolense, where many,
many people greeted it with applaude [sic].
The scene [. . .]. After the first waves of
applause, Dr. Roberto Maurino stated: "He
got by the best he could, almost always suffering, and he left the same way because he
got the worst of it in his last moments. Now,
for eternity, into the unknown, Alberto will
rest in peace. It was a great honor to be his
friend." [. . .] The procession then finally
continued with hundreds of cars. [. . .]
When the procession arrived at the local
cemetery, several hundred residents walked
with Burdisso's coffin to its final resting
place. There "Chacho" Pron, with warm
and heartfelt words, also remembered Alicia Burdisso, Alberto's sister, disappeared
on the twenty-first of June of 1976 during
the military Process [sic], in the province of
Tucumán.

40

That's it, I said to myself, interrupting my reading,
that's the reason my father decided to gather all this
information: symmetry. First a woman disappears,
then a man, and they are siblings and my father
perhaps knew them both and hadn't been able to

stop the disappearance of either one. But how could he? With what power did my father think he could prevent those disappearances—he who was dying in a hospital bed while I read all this?

41

"A mail [*sic*] has been released from custody, which doesn't mean that he won't be brought to trial. The case is being worked on throughout the whole region and the suspects are being held in the city of El Trébol and the Sastre jail. Important details were added in recent hours."

[. . .]

"Could Burdisso have been strangled?"

"We will know in the coming hours but we cannot corroborate it."

"Did he die in the well or before?"

"We are waiting for the results of the autopsy and the forensic report to determine this."

"In what state was the body? Did it have wounds or bruises?"

"The body was beaten. They did not find bullet entry wounds."

"Is there any relation among those arrested?"

"The suspects are related. Some closely and others allegedly."

[. . .]

42

The next day, a headline on the same website announced: "Alberto Burdisso Died by Suffocation and Was Savagely Beaten."

> The case was changed to Homicide by Criminal Trial Judge Dr. Eladio García[,] of the city of San Jorge. The forensic examination present that Burdisso presented [*sic*] a very hard blow to the head, perhaps caused by a blunt object, and numerous punches. He would have been thrown into the well while still alive.

43

More headlines: "El Trébol, Seven Arrests for the Burdisso Case" (*La Capital de *osario,* June 25); "A New Arrest in the Burdisso Case" (*El Trébol*

Digital, June 25); "Readers Applaud Treatment of the Burdisso Case" (*El Trébol Digital*, June 25); "Police Are Seeing Results in the Burdisso Case" (*El Trébol Digital*, June 26); "They Will Demand Justice in the Plaza" (*El Trébol Digital*, June 26). And one more headline, from the article that tells the whole story, published by *El Trébol Digital* the following day: "Burdisso Suffered Up Until His Final Moments."

44

The brutally murdered resident of El Trébol died, as detailed by the autopsy, of suffocation. His body was found with six broken ribs, the arm and shoulder fractured by the fall into the well. Alberto, according to declarations, was taken to the field on Sunday June 1rd [*sic*] at seven in the morning to look for firewood and there they beat him and threw him into the old well where he was found. Before throwing him into the well, they tried to make him sign a sales contract and he refused. According to the work by the forensic doctors and the autopsy, Alberto Burdisso recovered consciousness in the well but later died from asphyxia, though it remains unknown whether this was caused by his position in the well or from lack of air. The cellular telephone will play an important role in the trial,

since it was found along with Burdisso's body
and there are compromising called persons.

El Trébol Digital, June 27, 2008

45

If one reads the articles carefully and ignores
their typographical errors and erratic syntax, and
if afterward one thinks about what they say and
accepts that what they describe is what really must
have happened, one can sum up the entire story
in a more or less coherent narrative: A man was
taken to an isolated place through some kind of
deception and there he was ordered to sign over
an unknown property, which he refused to do; his
attackers threw him into a well and he died there.
In its simplicity, in its almost brutal pettiness, the
story could fit perfectly into one of those books of
the Old Testament in which the characters live
and, above all, die beholden to simple passions, by
the hand of an incomprehensible god who is nonetheless still worthy of praise and worship. However, since we can assume that this is not a biblical
story and that the motivations of the characters
are not subject to the whims of a capricious god,
when reading all this, we must also ask ourselves
what were the reasons behind these acts: Why was
this crime committed? How is it possible that so

many people are implicated in a murder that could have been carried out by one, two or, at the most, three people, all of whom could have fit in Burdisso's little car? And why was he murdered? For his house, which the anonymous writer at *El Trébol Digital* presented in his or her articles as a place with no particularly special features? It certainly wasn't some luxurious mansion that stood out in the puritanical, austere atmosphere of the town. For money? Where was this money going to come from, a sum large enough to outweigh the risk for his killers of winding up in prison for the rest of their lives? Where was a maintenance employee of an athletic club in a provincial town going to get all that money? How could Burdisso's suffocation be explained if the well, as first reported, was dry? Why didn't Burdisso call for help with his cell phone if it was found beside his body in the well? And who is compromised by the calls recorded by the cell phone, Burdisso or his murderers? Were the calls made before or after his fall into the well? Once again, who would want to kill some sort of Faulknerian fool, poorer than a church mouse, in a town where his disappearance would be noticed immediately, a town where, moreover, many people would know who Burdisso was, what he had done and who was with him in his final hours?

46

An article on June 27 by Claudio Berón, a journalist for *La Capital de *osario,* answered—to the
extent that these things can be answered—some
of these questions. I read it hastily:

> Finally, after three weeks of intense inves-
> tigations, the crime of Alberto Burdisso of
> El Treból was resolved. Burdisso, the 60-year-
> old man who [. . .] and whose cadaver was
> [. . .]. Gisela Córdoba, Gabriel Córdoba—
> her brother, Juan Huck and Marcos Bro-
> chero remained in custody charged with
> homicide. The motive, according to court
> sources, could be that they wanted Burdisso
> to sign a document leaving his house in Cór-
> doba's name, and when he refused they
> decided to kill him. After weighing various
> hypotheses, Criminal Judge Eladio García,
> who headed the investigation, decided to
> charge the four suspects and [. . .]. The
> Commissioner of the 18th Regional Unit,
> Jorge Gómez, also worked on the investiga-
> tion, mobilizing the Forensics Department
> of Rosario and Santa Fe, the canine divi-
> sion, which participated in the search for
> the body, and finally the Special Operations
> Troop (TOE). [. . .] It seems that Córdoba
> maintained a relationship with Huck while

at the same time saying that she was Burdisso's girlfriend. Huck and Córdoba seem to have taken the victim under false pretenses to the well where he was found. Brochero, Córdoba's legal spouse, would have later hidden the cadaver.

[. . .] The disappearance of Alberto José Burdisso shocked the city from the first moment [. . .] he missed work on June 2, a fact [. . .] also his debit card was found in the cash machine of Banco Nación, which had "swallowed" it the previous Saturday. [. . .] In addition, and as was repeatedly mentioned during the days he remained missing, he spent his money on women of easy virtue. [. . .] The worry and the conjectures about his [. . .] These demands grew so insistent that on Monday, June 16, fifteen days after his disappearance, a demonstration was organized to ask for an escalation of police efforts to find Burdisso. On that occasion, close to a thousand [. . .] and they signed a list of demands to request that Judge García consider the case a murder investigation.

Finally, the body was found on the 20th of this month. It was in a well on the property of a derelict home, some seven kilometers northeast of the city center. Around ten, after three hours of searching, a squadron of Volunteer Firemen discovered the body in an advanced state of decomposition at the bottom of the well, currently dry. As was published in *La Capital* in their edition of the 21st, the body was covered with rubble, corrugated metal sheets and branches, so the police ruled out a suicide or an accident.

The investigators arrived on the scene after a call from a hunter, who reported the day before that he had detected a strong odor in the area around the well. When they removed the cadaver—work that had to be done with pulleys and a tripod—they verified that it was wearing a shirt from the club. Other characteristics of the body, such as the large scar on the torso, led them to presume that it was the missing man. Nevertheless, this was confirmed a day later, when the body was subjected to an autopsy. [. . .] determined that the man had been in the early stages of asphyxia and had suffered hard blows to the head, but that he died inside the well.

Burdisso was buried last Sunday. His remains were accompanied by a procession of some 20 blocks and passed the headquarters of the club where he worked. It was in the late afternoon. Prior to that, there was a prayer for the dead in the parish of Saint Lawrence the Martyr.

The imminent arrest of a series of suspects was immediately made known. On Wednesday eight arrests had already been made. But in the end four individuals were charged, who remain in custody. [. . .] Those who knew him maintain that Burdisso was in general a withdrawn and gullible man who believed each one of the cunning arguments with which Córdoba deceived him.

So much so that one of the accused, Marcos Brochero, a native of Cañada Rosquín, was Córdoba's husband but Burdisso thought he was her brother.

47

In the photocopy of the article that appeared in his file, my father had highlighted in fluorescent yellow a paragraph I had missed in my reading and which he, a much better journalist than I—he in fact taught the journalists who in time would be my own teachers, in an almost preindustrial system of apprenticeship that in both form and content radically opposed the nonsense they tried to teach us at the university and, furthermore, bonded my father and me in a sort of involuntary tradition, an old school of rigorous and willful and defeated journalists—my father, as I was saying, had highlighted:

Burdisso had surrounded himself with a series of individuals from the margins of society, many of them with criminal records [. . .] he was 60 years old and lived alone in his house at 400 Calle Corrientes, four blocks from the club. He had no immediate family, since his sister had disappeared during the military dictatorship. For that loss [. . .] two years ago he received an indemnity from the state of 240 thousand pesos (some 56 thousand dollars). With that money he bought a house—the one they had wanted to take from him—a car, a motorcycle and other items.

48

Ten years ago, the towns on Route 13 were, to some, the gates to a lost paradise. Brothels, gambling and sex, both cheap and expensive. Nightclubs and all kinds of crime. That was, according to the sources consulted, up until two years ago. There were some forty brothels in the area and a lot of trafficking of women from Brazil and remote regions of Paraguay. Many of these women told the court of their trips to Europe to prostitute themselves.

Miriam Carizo was the owner of a bar of ill repute, where she met Alberto Burdisso in 2005 and struck up a relationship with him that lasted two years. Gisela Córdoba (28 years old), the woman Burdisso was involved with when his romance with Carizo ended, is believed to be part of this network and had prior convictions for check fraud in El Trébol itself. The other charged suspects were habitués of nightclubs. According to investigators on the case thus [*sic*] would be the "tail end" of these rings, which had already disappeared but left behind a saga of survivors of this life of vice.

A contextualization by Claudio Berón
in *La Capital de *osario,* June 29, 2008

49

A house, a lot of money that paradoxically was not the bearer of good fortune and an immense loneliness ended the life of Alberto Burdisso. [. . .] They killed him on the first Sunday of June. It is believed that a woman of ill repute wanted to take his property and for that she convinced two men and some other people of the need to have him disappear. [. . .] Several meters from the vast field that surrounds El Trébol, a town of no more than 13 thousand inhabitants, there is a new white house. There lived Burdisso; a man different from the rest, 60 years old and, according to some who knew him, celibate until the age of 57. In 2005 he received more than 200 thousand pesos in reparations for his disappeared younger sister. He burned through that cash.

According to Roberto Maurino, Burdisso was a sullen and withdrawn man, but normal. "He traveled alone and only to the south. We had a lot of chats. He finished school and then worked at the Club Trebolense. With the cash he got, he bought a house in Rosario, a house here and an old car. He was too trusting," he declared. Around the time of the compensation he met a woman, Miriam Carizo. He bought a house and put it in both of their names, he gave her a car and, his coworkers say, he paid for a birthday party for her daughter, with whom he had an almost paternal relationship. "Burdi was like that, just crazy. He said everybody does what they want with their lives. He talked a lot to people he wanted to talk to. He didn't bother nobody. He had his paycheck held to cover the loans they made him take out. We're grieving for him. He surrounded himself with bad people. And who knows why they killed him, they even had control of his paychecks," they say at the club.

For a long time along Route 13 there were prostitution rings and other dubious activity. Close to 40 brothels were opened in towns like El Trébol, San Jorge, Sastre and others in the district of General San Martín. "It's all connected, this is the tail end of a story of shady characters," suggested investigators. [. . .] Burdi had ended things with Carizo and met Gisela Córdoba, a woman battered by life, hardened by its absolute lack of charity. Córdoba has three children and lives with her legal husband, Marcos Brochero, but had, apparently, a relationship with two "boyfriends," Burdi and a 64-year-old man, Juan Huck, who she met in one of these establishments of easy virtue. Doubts about her motive turned to certainty over the course of the investigation. "Statements were taken from the eight charged suspects, including Gisela Córdoba, Juan Huck, Marcos Brochero and Gabriel Córdoba, who remained under arrest for suspicion of homicide," they said. The issue turned out to be the house co-owned by Burdisso and Miriam Carizo. Carizo, about 40 years old, married another man, but Burdi stayed in the house. Gisela Córdoba knew about the property and got Burdisso to put half in her name, though he retained the legal right to live there. He had to die or disappear in order for Córdoba to occupy the house or sell it.

They took him to a deserted area and tried to force him to sign a document to free up the property. Days earlier, Córdoba had consulted lawyers on how to deal with Burdisso's rights to the house in the case of his disappearance. Furthermore, it seems that she already had put the house up for rent. [. . .] After his death, Burdi received a fond farewell at the doors of the club where he worked. At the reception desk there is a letter: "I wanted to tell you that Ñafa put your bike away, that you are missed and that Ana is inconsolable. Your dog keeps looking for you and crying." It is signed by Laura Maurino.

Claudio Berón in
La Capital de *osario, June 29, 2008

50

In one of the photographs that accompanied the article you can see a one-story house behind a tiny parcel of lawn on an unpaved, sewerless street. The house has a large two-paned window and another smaller one at the entrance, which has its own small roof held up by a fragile-looking column. In front of the house there is a hedge, but it seems to have dried up. The house is shuttered and, strangely, it looks like there is a high-backed chair lying facedown on a stretch of open ground, a plot of land where no one is ever going to live. That's the house they killed Alberto Burdisso for.

51

Looking up from my father's file, I gazed out at the courtyard of the house he'd built and wondered what he had said at Burdisso's funeral, if he was there when the body was found in that well and if there was something my father knew or could know and I would never know, something having to do with the sordid, sad backdrop of a town that I had believed idyllic. In that courtyard before my eyes, I'd played games I no longer remember, games that came from the books I read and the films I saw and, particularly, from a period of sadness and terror that now, slowly, was coming back in spite of all the pills, my memory loss and the distance I'd tried to put between myself and that time. Burdisso's corpse was pulled from the well using a tripod and pulleys, said the article, and I wondered if my father had been there at that moment, if my father had seen the body of the brother of someone who had been his friend hanging from a hook like an animal, floating above the town, already definitively sullied by vice. I also wondered if the story had ended, if I would find out what had happened to Burdisso's murderers and if the symmetry in this story had already run out, the lines moving away from each other, vanishing into space, which is infinite, and, therefore, meeting up again somewhere. I wondered if my father could think about these things in a hospital bed, unreachable to me but not to the past; soon to be part of the past himself.

52

Some two hundred residents gathered in El Trébol's Plaza San Martín on Sunday afternoon to demand the sentencing of the killers in the Burdisso case. There, Dr. Roberto Maurino [. . .] explained the situation of the four in custody and the latest news of the trial: "The case is not closed. There are four suspects charged with obligatory jail time. There is no bail set for them and they will have to endure the process from the inside. Later will come the trial in Santa Fe, where they will be condemned or absolved. Of the four detainees, three are accused of premeditated homicide acting as a group or a gang, and the fourth as a secondary participant with a sentence of fifteen to twenty years. The maximum penalty for the first three is life imprisonment. [. . .] Of the suspects who have been released, three are charged with aggravated concealment, which is to say, they knew but said nothing. I do not know whom [sic] they are. Their charge does not carry a minimum jail sentence and they can go free at the discretion of the court. [. . .] The four detainees confessed their guilt. We will now search, as a town, as a civil association or as a club, for a plaintiff to participate in the trial. To date the law has only allowed this in one case: the Mothers of the Plaza de Mayo against a torturer. The idea is to keep tabs on the case in the Sentencing Court of Santa Fe."

El Trébol Digital, June 30, 2008

53

At the bottom of the article there was a photograph showing a group of people around an old man holding up a megaphone with his back to the photographer; in the background, to the left, I thought I recognized my father.

54

Next in the file were two letters to the editor addressed to *El Trébol Digital,* one signed by a woman whose last name was Bianchini and another by a ten-year-old girl. A week later, on July 7, the news was published of a demonstration in which some forty-two people had called for the killers' sentencing; in the photos that followed I didn't see my father. Then there was a photocopy of the front page of a newspaper I'd never seen before, *El Informativo,* showing a photograph of two policemen escorting a man, with a jacket covering his face, from a car. "The Murderers Could Get Life in Prison" was the headline, accompanied by the following teasers at the bottom of the page: "The untold side of the story. Who was Alberto Burdisso?

Why did they kill him? Chronicle of a tragic end. The story of his sister. The clairvoyant that foresaw his reappearance."

55

The next article, which summed up the story in a profusion of yellow journalism, littered with superfluous commas that brought to mind a fetid flower, was signed by Francisco Díaz de Azevedo. An excerpt:

[. . .] in the house on Corrientes, number 438, which he had bought and put under his name and that of his ex common-law wife, a few years earlier, and from which he had been evicted and left to live practically abandoned in a garage.

[. . .] For some time now, another woman kept his entire monthly salary, in exchange for temporary companionship, and, recently, she had even gotten him into several fights. In fact, Alberto hadn't frequented the house of this new "companion" in three months, because he had had an altercation that came to blows with this woman's common-law husband, a fact that is confirmed by the police; which is why she was the one that went to Burdisso's house, "to visit."

As regards Alberto's economic situation, the money that he received in 2006, for the death of his sister during the Process (220,000 pesos), absolutely nothing remained of it.

On the afternoon of Saturday the 31st, and contrary to what was said and assumed, Alberto Burdisso withdrew all the money of his salary, via the cash machine of Banco Nación, since on the last business day of the month, Trebolense had deposited his salary. Afterward, his card was held in the bank itself, although nobody knows what later happened to that money, since it never appeared again. The next day, at approximately seven thirty in the morning, Burdisso was picked up at his domicile on Calle Corrientes, by a male and a woman, to go look for wood in a field bordering the city. When they arrived at the abandoned house, Burdi's escorts sought to pressure him into signing a series of papers and documents regarding his home, which he resisted, and it was then that he was thrown into a dry well, of some ten meters deep.

In the fall, the victim suffered six broken ribs, a broken arm and shoulder, but he remained alive, in that place. That same evening, Burdi's cell phone received, in the depths of the well, calls from relatives of the woman who went there with him and with whom he had occasional relations. The calls were to check if he was still alive.

The following day, Monday July 1st, the common-law husband of the woman who threw the resident into the well, arrived at the field, tore down the stonework from around the well and threw metal sheets and tree trunks onto the humanity [sic] of Alberto. Shortly after this fact, his death is produced by suffocation and confinement. Which is to say, Burdi was alive for at least twenty-four hours in the well and only died after being covered by the refuse.

For twenty days, the searches were un-fruitful and almost useless. Until one after-noon, the city police station, received the information that Burdisso could have been thrown into a well, in the rural area. [. . .] This person, indicated three possible loca-tions and accompanied police personnel to visit them, detecting, that one of the wells (in which he was finally found), wasn't in the same shape, as the last time this "woodsman" had seen it, detecting with his bare eyes, that some stonework around the top of the well was missing. [. . .] It was fireman Javier Ber-gamasco, who from inside the hole, noticed that there was a body, in an advanced state of decomposition. He proceeded with a *'prima facie'* examination with Dr. Pablo Candiz, at the site of the finding and later in the El Trébol morgue, where coworkers and friends, identified him by the particular scar he had on his abdomen. [. . .] The autopsy revealed that Alberto had been beaten about the eyes and behind the ears, with, surely, fists, before being thrown into the well.

Automatically, after the finding of the body, they carried out a string of simultaneous arrests, after a week of witness statements, they will go to trial: a woman, Gisela C., twenty-seven years old, who already had priors for fraud, Juan H., sixty-three years old, with no prior convictions, Marcos B., thirty-one years old, with priors for drug consumption and the common-law husband of Gisela C. and Gabriel C., thirty-four years old, brother of Gisela C. with priors for misdemeanor theft [. . .].

56

When I reached this point, I went back a few pages and again unfolded the map my father had used, but I didn't know how to find out if any of the rural homes he'd visited and marked on the map was the house where the murder had taken place, and, in that case, if it had been my father who had alerted the police. On a small blank page I found on my father's desk I jotted down: "Was my father the firewood collector—the hunter, in other versions—who filed the report with the police?" and I remained contemplating what I'd written for a long while. Finally I turned the page over and discovered that it was an invoice for some photographic enlargements that weren't in the file but—though I didn't know yet, so I should pretend here that I don't know—were inside another of the files piled up on the desk, to which I would return time and time again in the days following these discoveries.

57

"How long have you lived in El Trébol?"

"About twenty years."

"What are you?"

"I belong to a charismatic center. I've been strengthening the mental part."

"Are you clairvoyant?"

"I haven't gotten that far."

"Are you a witch?"

"No."

"Do they call you a witch?"

"Affectionately. Witch, witchy and crone."

"Do you make your living this way?"

"I have up until now."

"Describe to me what your powers are."

"I channel myself to help those who need it for good. I channel for health, work and affection."

"How does that include the Burdisso case?"

"I measured myself. I wanted to see my ability and my reach."

"What did you see?"

"The first Monday he disappeared, I saw that he was still alive. It was that Monday. The following days it was already looking more doubtful. It could be or not. I saw all the ups and downs. Then, it gave me [sic] that he was deceased. That he could be in a place with stagnant water, depth, a sewer, a well, et cetera. It wasn't clear. But they were looking in the cemetery and I felt that wasn't right."

"What did you feel when the case was solved?"

"Very powerless because this is a small town. Very annoyed. [. . .] I couldn't help him in the moments that he manifested himself to me that he was alive. I don't knew [sic] whether to call it strength or coward-ice, because I didn't come forward in those moments and I didn't reveal myself, I didn't reveal my ability to help."

"How do you see these things?"

"Through writings. I call it 'mermerism' [sic] and it is through the fingertips. I carve around and I look at the contents of the person, but I never let the person tell me about their situation directly. I try to decipher it myself [. . .]."

58

Alberto's mother died when he was very young and he never talked about her, I guess he didn't remember her. [. . .] His father went missing when he was only fifteen years old, and at that point Burdi was already doing jobs as a laborer and bricklayer's assistant. He lived a life of loneliness, humility and simplicity, and we should acknowledge him as one of those people behind the scenes in this country. Who live silently, scraping by, in a highly complicated society. [. . .] [In the late 1970s] he told me about the problem with his sister, [. . .] and I went with him to Tucumán, but, unfortunately, we returned empty-handed. [. . .] That money [the reparations given by the state as compensation for being a relative of a disappeared person] doomed him, in every sense. His life was, without a doubt, torturous. His childhood was marked by the absence of his mom. As a teenager his father dies. Then, the only loved one he has left, his sister, is murdered by the military dictatorship and, when he gets some financial stability, which could have allowed him to enjoy life, he ends up losing everything, even life itself. Burdi could have left the money in the Club's mutual fund and lived off the interest. But we advised him to buy property, it seemed to us the best way to invest some of the money and, besides, he would have a place of his own to live. Maybe if we'd made a different suggestion, this wouldn't have happened.

Roberto Maurino, childhood friend of
Alberto Burdisso, in statements to
El Informativo, El Trébol, July 2008

59

Next in my father's file was a page titled simply "Fanny," and undated:

A civilian plaintiff is needed as a driving force in the criminal proceedings. This is the task assigned to the district attorney, but the civilian plaintiff intervenes to guarantee that he won't let the proceedings stagnate. There was an attempt to convince some cousins from El Trébol, but they are avoiding committing to it. The civil plaintiff will be assisted by a lawyer from Santa Fe (where the sentence will be handed down) who is the grandson of Luciano Molinas and an activist in the association HIJOS [acronym for Children United for Identification and Justice and Against Forgetting and Silence, an organization of the children of Argentine disappeared]. This lawyer has experience in the matter and has agreed to charge

minimal fees, to which will be added the
expenses required for the court filing (where
this money will come from is something
that has to be discussed). The inheritance
of the property on Calle Corrientes, whose
undivided half share is registered in Alberto's
name, should also be dealt with at this time.

60

Following that was an article from the August 1 edition of the newspaper *El Ciudadano & La Región,*
from *osario, titled "Criminal Conspiracy." I didn't
need to read past the first line to know that my
father had written it. A paragraph:

> The couple planned and executed the sin-
> ister plot over a year and a half, according
> to the judicial investigation. The fatal victim
> was Alberto Burdisso, a sixty-year-old man
> who lived in the town of El Trébol and had
> received reparations of two hundred thou-
> sand pesos. The man entered into a romantic
> relationship with Gisela Córdoba, thirty-
> three years his junior, and gradually handed
> over to her: half of his house (since the other
> half belonged to his ex-wife), furniture, a car
> and a large part of his monthly earnings. He
> even moved into the garage, leaving the
> house in the hands of the young woman

(who rented it out the same day Burdisso was pushed into the well where he lay dying for three days), just as he found out that the young woman's supposed brother was actually her husband. Meanwhile, the girl picked up a new lover, sixty-three years old, who ended up involved in the crime. The motive was a supposed life insurance policy that she believed was in her name.

An article in *La Capital de *osario* dated that same day with the byline Luis Emilio Blanco below the title "El Trébol: They Prosecute Burdisso's Killers and Reveal Details of the Case" did not contribute any additional information but did offer slightly different facts: Here Burdisso is sixty-one and not sixty, Marcos Brochero is thirty-two and not thirty-one, Juan Huck is sixty-one and not sixty-three, the abandoned rural house where the body was found is eight and not nine kilometers from town (in a piece published the next day in the newspaper *El Litoral* of Santa Fe, the distance was reduced to six kilometers). Here it is Gisela Córdoba and not Juan Huck who threw the man into a well that's twelve and not ten meters deep, Burdisso broke five ribs and not six and both shoulders instead of a shoulder and an arm, as in the previous version, but those are all minor details. More interesting is the supposed request from Córdoba to Huck to "get him out of the well and throw him somewhere so they'll find him and confirm his death" to enable her to gain access to the life insurance she believed was in her name; Huck refused. The article also included some secondary information revealed in the autopsy: "[. . .] the results show that the man had dirt in his mouth and respiratory tract, which indicates that he tried to breathe beneath the material thrown onto him," specified the source.

61

Whether it was Brochero, who, in some versions, had stayed in El Trébol that morning, whether it was Córdoba, or whether it was Huck, who maintains that he was a victim in all this—who threw Burdisso into the well is of little importance here; nor does it matter much that Brochero returned three days later to throw bricks, pieces of masonry and dead leaves onto the wounded man to finish him off; the fate of the accused doesn't matter much, and neither does what happened to Córdoba in the women's prison in Santa Fe or to Brochero and Huck in the jail in Coronda. This crime, every crime, has an individual, private aspect but also a social one; the first concerns only the victims and their close relatives, but the second concerns us all and is the reason justice is required to intervene in our name, in the name of a collective whose rules have been called into question by the crime and which, faced with the impossibility of undoing the first, tries to get the second under control, with power that, at least in theory, comes neither from an individual nor a single class but rather from society as a whole, wounded but still standing.

62

The remaining questions at that point were who Fanny was, why my father summed up the case's legal situation and why it was my father who had to do it and not someone else, anyone else.

63

The next documents in my father's file were fragments of a register I didn't recognize, in which appeared people with the last name Carizo, including Miriam, Burdisso's common-law wife to whom he'd given fifty percent of his property, which was documented here with one new detail: Burdisso's and her tax and national identification numbers. Then there was a photocopy of the document produced by the General Property Registry of the

Province of Santa Fe, detailing the purchase of the house on Calle Corrientes by Alberto Burdisso and dating the purchase to November 16, 2005. Burdisso had bought the property from Nelson Carlos Girello and Olga Rosa Capitani de Girello, two elderly people. Other information was included on the bill of sale: Burdisso's birth date—February 1, 1948; his mother's last name—Rolotti; marital status—single; his national identification card number—6.309.907; and his previous address—Entre Ríos and Cortada Llobet, in El Trébol. Also the size of the property—307.20 square meters; and the amount paid—twenty-five thousand pesos in cash. The notary public who had witnessed the transaction was named Ricardo López de la Torre.

64

It was as if my father had wanted to deconstruct the crime into a handful of insignificant facts, a pile of notarized documents, technical descriptions and official registries whose accumulation made him forget for a moment that they all added up to a tragic event, the disappearance and death of a man in an abandoned well, which would make him think about the symmetry between that man's death and his sister's, also tragic and about which my father was never going to know anything. This was my father's attempt to collaborate in the search for Burdisso and my attempt to search for and find my father in his last thoughts before everything that had happened happened.

65

[. . .] that they sell to Mr. Alberto José Burdisso and Mrs. Miriam Emilia Carizo, in joint ownership of indivisible, equal parts: a plot of land including everything constructed or planted on it, located in the city of El Trébol, District San Martín, part of the block numbered Seventy-Eight on the official map. [. . .] said map is registered in the Topographical Department under number 130,355, dated the 18th of February of 2000, attached here, and said portion is designated as lot number six (6), located on the North part of the block, divided by a public walkway, situated at twenty-five meters eight centimeters from the Northeast corner of the block toward the East, and composed of: twelve meters eighty centimeters facing North, the same facing South, by twenty-four meters on its East and West sides, equivalent to an area of three hundred seven meters twenty decimeters square, adjoining: to the North, Calle Corrientes; to the West, lot number Five; to the East, lot number Seven; and to the

South, lot number Eleven, all on the same map of measurement.

66

El Trébol, June 9, 2008, 10:30 time [*sic*]. REGARDING: It being the date and time that figure on the margin, a person of the female sex appears before this Police Station wishing to file civil record, a request immediately accepted. Next is gathered her full names and other circumstances relating to her personal identity[.] LET THE RECORD STATE that she gave her name as: MIRIAM EMILIA CARIZO, Argentine, educated, single, employed, National Identification Number [. . .], residenced in a rural region in the mid-East, who being found competent for the function STATES: "That she is the co-owner of the dwelling located on Calle Corrientes number 438 along with Mr. Alberto José Burdisso, and, in the face of his absence and under advisement by the Court of this city, asks to change the locks of the dwelling in the evening hours if possible to prevent a possible usurpation. That is all. The present record states for legal purposes that this is not to be interpreted as home abandonment, rather due to the circumstances aforementioned. The above is all I have to say on the subject, having nothing more to add, delete or amend . . ." As that is all, the record is considered completed, read and ratified by the declarant signing below in accordance before I [*sic*] who certifies. SIGNED: Miriam Emilia Carizo (declarant). Agent (S.G.) María Rosa Finos, acting police officer. I HEREBY CERTIFY: that the present record is a faithful copy of the existing original found on page 12 in the [. . .].

67

Then my father had drawn Burdisso's family tree, starting with his grandparents, including dates only for the births and deaths of Alberto and Alicia. For Alicia, the second date, the date of her death, appears as a question mark.

69

A photograph showing an oval portrait of a man with a Nietzschean mustache and a bow tie beside a plaque: "Jorge Burdisso † 2.19.1928 aged 72. In remembrance by his family." Another photograph: "Margarita G. de Burdisso † 3.31.1933 aged 68. In remembrance by her family." A photograph of a vault, with the inscription "Burdisso Family." When I saw that photograph, I jumped, because I knew that vault: I had hidden behind it and other similar tombs, playing hide-and-seek in the cemetery with my friends when there were no adults around.

70

A photocopy of a list of telephone numbers and contact information for people with the last name Páez and for the perfume shop Fanny.

71

The last page in the file was titled "A Eulogy for Alberto José Burdisso" and was dated "El Trébol Cemetery, June 21, 2008." It was a transcription of the words my father spoke at the funeral of Alberto José Burdisso:

Friends and neighbors, there is not much I can add to what has already been said. You surely knew Alberto better than I did, as we were friends for only a few months during primary school.

But I felt obliged to come here with

him and with you in order to give voice to someone who could not be here today. The entire town should be here, because I don't believe Alberto brought anything but good into anyone's life. And many have come. Those taken first from this world, like his parents and his aunt, who raised him, aren't here. The indifferent aren't here, those who live gazing at their own navels, oblivious to everything beyond their own interests. And someone in particular isn't here. Someone who is nowhere yet everywhere, waiting for the truth, calling for justice, demanding remembrance.

That person is Alicia, Alberto's sister, who in spite of being younger looked after him like an older sister when they were left alone.

But Alicia isn't here, hasn't been here for thirty-one years. It is exactly thirty-one years to the day that she was disappeared in Tucumán, on June 21, 1977, by the thugs of the most recent and the bloodiest civil-military dictatorship.

Alicia was kidnapped and disappeared because she was part of a generation that had to fight to restore freedom to our country. So people like Alberto and like all of us could live in a world without fear and without gags in our mouths. Without those young people like Alicia, today we wouldn't be able to say what we think, act as we feel we should, choose our destiny. For example, our march to the plaza to demand Alberto be found would not be possible. Nor would the demonstrations of the last few days during which people have been able to speak out about the kind of country they want without fear of being kidnapped and disappeared.

Today we say good-bye to Alberto in a way we were unable to with Alicia. Which is why I ask that when you demand justice for him, remember to demand it for her as well. And may the Lord receive the spirits of them both among his chosen ones.

72

Next there was a blank page, and then nothing except for the porous surface of the file's yellow cardboard, which remained open for a moment and then was closed by a hand that, although at that moment I wasn't thinking about it at all, belonged to me and was covered in folds and grooves like country roads traveled by devastation and death.

Parents are the bones children sharpen their teeth on.

—Juan Domingo Perón

1

Once, a long time before any of this happened, my mother gave me a jigsaw puzzle that I rushed to put together while she watched. It probably didn't take me very long, since it was a puzzle for kids and had few pieces, no more than fifty. When I finished, I brought it to my father and showed it to him with childish pride, but my father shook his head and said, It's very easy, and asked me to give it to him. I handed over the puzzle and he started to cut the pieces into tiny bits devoid of any meaning. He didn't stop until he had cut up every one of the pieces, and when he was done he said to me: Put it together now. But I was never able to do it again. Several years earlier, my father, instead of destroying a puzzle, had made one for me, with wooden pieces that were rectangular, square, triangular and round, which he painted different colors to make them easier to identify; of all the pieces, I vaguely remember that the round ones were yellow and the square ones were maybe red or blue, but what's important here is that, as I closed my father's file, I began to think he'd created yet another puzzle for me. This time, however, the pieces were movable and had to be assembled on a larger tabletop that was memory and in fact the world. Once again, I wondered why my father had participated in the search for that murdered man, why he'd wanted to document his efforts and the results that they'd failed to produce, as well as the final words he'd said on the subject, linking the murdered man with his disappeared sister. I had the impression that my father hadn't really been looking for the dead man, who meant little or nothing to him; that what he'd been doing was searching for the sister, picking up a search that certain tragic circumstances—which I myself, and perhaps he and my mother, had tried to forget—had kept him from carrying out in June 1977, when he and my mother and I—my siblings had not yet been born—lived in a state of terror that delayed sounds and movements from reaching us, as if we were underwater. I told myself that my father had wanted to find his friend through her brother, but I also wondered why he hadn't begun that search sooner, when the murdered brother was still alive and it wouldn't have been difficult for my father to talk to him; when the brother went missing, I thought, one of the last bonds linking my father to the disappeared woman was broken, and precisely because of that it made no sense to search for him, given that the dead don't talk, they say nothing from the depths of the wells they've been thrown into out on the Argentine plain. I wondered if my father knew his search wouldn't turn up any results, if he was simply captivated by the symmetry of two missing siblings with more than thirty years between them, willing to throw himself again and again at a light that dazzled him until he collapsed from exhaustion, like an insect in the dark, hot air of a summer night.

3

My sister was standing beside the coffee machine at one end of the hallway in the intensive care unit and spoke only when I finished telling her about my father's file. He participated in the search for Burdisso but he did it on his own, not getting involved in the other efforts, she told me. He looked in places that didn't interest the police, like gullies and streams, and beneath collapsed bridges; also in abandoned houses at the crossroads of country roads. Maybe he was already sick then, or maybe he got sick because of what happened. He talked of nothing else during all the weeks the search went on. I asked my sister why my father had gotten involved in a search for someone he barely knew, but my sister interrupted me with a gesture and said: He knew him; they went to school together at some point. For how long, I asked. My sister shrugged: I don't know, but once he told me that he regretted not having spoken to Burdisso about his sister while he was still alive, that he occasionally saw him on the street and always thought about approaching him to ask if he knew anything about her, but he couldn't think of a good way to start the conversation and ended up just letting it go. Who is Fanny, I asked. My sister thought for a minute: She's a distant relative of Burdisso. He tried to convince her to intervene in the trial as a civilian plaintiff to speed it along. What made him want to look for the missing girl, I asked, but my sister brought the cup of coffee to her lips, took a sip and tossed it in the wastepaper basket. It's cold, she murmured and took another coin out of her pocket and put it into the machine and said, as if continuing a previous conversation: You saw him in the museum. Who, I asked. My sister said my father's name. They interviewed him for an exhibition in the municipal museum; you should go see it, she added, and I nodded in silence.

3

When I entered the museum, I paid my admission and looked around for the exhibition on the local daily press. The museum brought together various insignificant miscellanea, the odds and ends of a mercantile city that lacked any history beyond the fluctuating prices of the grains unloaded over the years in its port, the only justification for its existence in that spot beside a river, not two kilometers farther south or north or any other place at all. As I walked through the museum, I thought about how I'd lived in that city and how at some point it had been the place where I was supposedly going to remain, permanently tied down by an atavistic force that no one seemed able to explain but that affected many people who lived there, who hated it vehemently and yet never left, a city that wouldn't release its hold on those born there, who traveled and came back or who never went anywhere and tanned in the summer and coughed in the winter and bought houses with their wives and had kids who were never able to leave the city either.

4

In the room that held the exhibition on the daily press there was a television on a constant loop, and a chair. I sat in it trembling, listening to data and figures and watching the front pages of newspapers until my father appeared on the screen. He was as I remembered him in his last years. He had a long white beard, which he occasionally ran his fingers through with a flirtatious air, and he talked about newspapers where he'd worked, newspapers he'd seen go under and reappear with other names and other staffs in other places that, invariably, were finished off by the courts soon afterward, so the newspapers went under again and the cycle repeated itself from the beginning, if there ever was one; a whole series of pretty terrible cycles of exploitation and unemployment following one after another without leaving any room for a career or for hope. My father told his story, which was also the story of the press in this city where he'd decided to live, and I, watching him on the screen at that museum exhibition, felt both pride and very strong disappointment, the same disappointment I usually felt when I thought about everything my father had done and the impossibility of following in his footsteps or of offering him achievements that could match his own, which were many and were counted in newspaper pages, in journalists trained by him who in turn had trained me and in a political history that I had once known and then tried to almost completely forget.

5

I watched the documentary that included the interview with my father three or four times that afternoon, listening to him attentively until I'd familiarized myself with all the dates and names but, more crucially, until looking at him started to be too terrible. I'm going to start crying, I thought, but thinking about it was enough to keep me from doing it. At some point an employee came in and announced that the exhibition would be closing in five minutes, and then he approached the television and turned it off. My father was cut off in the middle of a sentence, and I tried to finish it but couldn't: where my father's face had been I began to see mine, reflected in the black screen with all my features gathered in an expression of pain and sadness that I'd never seen before.

7

Once my father told me that he would have liked to write a novel. That night, at his desk, in a room that had once been mine and that never seemed to have enough light, I wondered if he hadn't actually done it. Among his papers was a list of names laid out in two columns, colored lines linking them in which red predominated. There was also a page from a newspaper, the front page of a local newspaper called *Semana Gráfica* that I knew—because I'd once heard my father say it, and what he'd said, particularly the pride with which he'd said it, had survived the almost total collapse of my memory— was a newspaper he'd created as a teenager and that had been his first job in journalism, long before he went to a city in the heart of the country to study that discipline. There were also photographs, and perhaps these were the materials for the novel my father had wanted to write and never did.

8

What must the novel my father wanted to write have been like? Brief, composed of fragments, with holes where my father couldn't or didn't want to remember something, filled with symmetries—stories duplicating themselves over and over again as if they were an ink stain on an assiduously folded piece of paper, a simple theme repeated as in a symphony or a fool's monologue—and sadder than Father's Day at an orphanage.

9

One thing was clear: the novel my father would have written wouldn't have been an allegory or domestic fiction or an adventure or a romance, it wouldn't have been a ballad or a coming-of-age novel, it wouldn't have been a detective novel or a fable or a fairy tale or historical fiction, it wouldn't have been a comic novel or an epic or a fantasy, not a gothic or an industrial novel; it certainly wouldn't have been a realist novel or a novel of ideas or a postmodern novel, not a newspaper serial or a novel in the nineteenth-century style; and there's no way it would have been a parable or science fiction, suspense or a social novel, a novel of chivalry or a bodice-ripper; while we're at it, it probably wouldn't have been a mystery or a horror novel either, even though those would cause the right amount of fear and grief.

10

Among my father's papers I found a paid announcement from the Argentine newspaper *Página/12* dated Thursday, June 27, 2002. The text of the announcement:

> Alicia Raquel Burdisso, journalist, university student in literature (25 years old). Arrested/disappeared by security forces in the city of Tucumán on 6-21-77.
>
> It has been 25 years since her kidnapping (as she left work), and we still do not know what happened. We cannot forget the sinister crime of her disappearance. We have never received any official explanation of this shameful crime.

We remember you with much affection
and feeling.
Alberto, Mirta, Fani, David

To the right of the text there was a photograph of
a young woman. She had an oval face framed by
thick black hair, her thin eyebrows prominent and
her large eyes heavily outlined in eyeliner, not looking at the viewer but beyond, at someone or something located to the right and above wherever the
anonymous photographer was when he or she took
the picture of this woman, her thin lips twisted
into an expression of interrogatory seriousness.
There was no reason to doubt that the woman in
the photograph was Alicia Raquel Burdisso; what's
more, everything seemed to point to that, but her
gaze and her unusual seriousness made it seem
as if she were no twenty-five-year-old but rather a
woman who had seen many things and decided to
press on toward them, someone who could barely
stop for a second to pose for a photograph, a person who concentrated so intensely on that point
above her that, if asked in the moment she was
being photographed, she would hardly have been
able to give her name or home address.

11

Then there were other photographs. The first showed a dozen young people sitting around a table with two bottles of wine, one of which was still unopened, and some glasses. Not all the young people looked at the photographer; only the one to the left of the young man who is my father, and two women standing behind him. A series of details, particularly the bars on a window, made me realize that the young people were in the living room of my paternal grandparents' house; two of them are holding guitars: my father, whose left hand is positioned in what seems to be an E chord at the top of the instrument's neck, and a young woman who seems to be playing a C minor chord—it also could be G-sharp minor; the lack of capo makes it hard to be sure—and looks toward the right of the photograph. My father and another young man are wearing plaid shirts; another, stripes; two women are wearing the kind of floral dresses common in the 1960s; two women have straight hair and another sports a haircut à la Jeanne Moreau. My father wears his hair long for the period, and a bushy beard that shows only his chin, which he must have shaved. Behind this group of young people is a chalkboard on which someone has written:

"*Semana Gráfica,* a year of venom." On the right side of the photograph is a young woman who is smiling and looking forward and seems to be singing. It's Alicia Raquel Burdisso.

12

Another photograph showed the same group of young people, joined by another, probably the photographer of the previous image, in the courtyard of my grandparents' house. One of them is smoking. My father smiles. Alicia leans on the shoulder of one of the women, who blocks her almost completely.

13

A third photograph showed them horsing around. My father is wearing some sort of helmet and holding up one wrist; Alicia is to his right and wears a straw hat and a flower in her hair; she is smoking and, for the first time in the series of photographs, laughing. The photograph is dated November 1969.

14

If you have a digital copy of the photograph, as I do, and if you enlarge it again and again, as my father did, the woman's face breaks down into a multitude of gray squares until the woman literally disappears.

15

My father had even written a brief biographical summary of the people linked with arrows on the first page of the file: there were names and dates and names of political parties and groups that no longer existed and whose memory reached me like the imaginary voices of the dead in a séance. My father's list included a dozen names, six of which were associated with names of political organizations. Then my father had included some photocopies of the first page of the publication he ran, and highlighted in yellow the names of people who appeared on the list. One of them was Alicia Raquel Burdisso, who, on my father's list, was reduced to a single date, that of her birth; in place of the other was a question mark, but for me, there and then, that question mark didn't introduce a question but rather an answer, an answer that explained everything.

16

Next there was a printout, presumably from the Internet, with the photograph from the commemorative paid announcement in *Página/12,* and the following text:

> Alicia Raquel Burdisso Rolotti: Arrested/ Disappeared on 6/21/77. Alicia was 25 years old. She was born on March 8, 1952. Student of journalism and literature. She wrote poems and articles for the magazine *Aquí Nosotras* of the UMA [Argentine Women's Union, the female section of the Communist Party]. And the newspaper *Nuestra Palabra* [historical and official organ of this Party]. She was kidnapped from her workplace in San Miguel de Tucumán. She was seen at the Clandestine Detention Center of the Tucumán Police Headquarters.

On the same page was a statement in the form of a letter to Alicia, signed by René Nuñez:

> Soul sister, I still remember when in the midst of the cold and the terrifying silence

I moved aside my blindfold and there you were, so little, so skinny that I thought you were a twelve-year-old girl, we greeted each other with a smile and I sensed an exceptional strength in you that filled me with hope, especially when you encouraged me and told me (with signs and silent writing on the wall) "from here they're taking us to the PEN [National Executive Branch], we're saved." I was sure it was all over because they were taking me to be executed, but they didn't kill me, I don't know why, they threw me into a wasteland filled with garbage. That's why my hopes were so high, I never imagined I wouldn't ever see you again. Sister, ally, comrade! I could do nothing more for you except remember you and keep spreading, in your name and in the name of all those who are no longer with us, the word of our struggle.

Then, finally, there was a poem:

> *Come, leave behind this daybreak*
> *your gaping holes and loneliness*
> *where egotism ran aground*
> *and devoured you, unforgivable.*
> *Then you'll see that your blindness was only*
> * mystical*
> *that there were shadows in your soul*
> *and that it is possible to reach the dawn*
> * together*
> *to see our new day.*

Maybe the poem was by Alicia Burdisso.

17

When I left the photographs on my father's desk, I understood that his interest in what had happened to Alberto Burdisso was the result of his interest in what had happened to Alberto's sister, Alicia, and that interest was in turn the product of a fact that perhaps my father couldn't even explain to himself but, in trying to, he had gathered all those materials. This fact was, my father had gotten Alicia involved in politics without knowing that what he was doing would cost that young woman her life, would cost him decades of fear and regret and would have its effects on me, many years later. As I tried to shift my attention from the photographs I'd just seen, I understood for the first time that all the children of young Argentines in the 1970s were going to have to solve our parents' pasts, like detectives, and what we would find out was going to seem like a mystery novel we wished we'd never bought. But I also realized that there was no way of telling my father's story as a mystery or, more precisely, that telling it in such a way would betray his intentions and his struggles, since telling his story as a detective tale would merely confirm the existence of a genre, which is to say, a convention, and all of his efforts were meant to call into question those very social conventions and their pale reflection in literature.

18

Besides, I'd seen enough mystery novels already and would see many more in the future. Telling this story from the perspective of genre would be illegitimate. To begin with, the individual crime was less important than the social crime, but social crime couldn't be told through the artifice of a detective novel; it needed a narrative in the shape of an enormous frieze or with the appearance of an intimate personal story that held something back, a piece of an unfinished puzzle that would force the reader to look for adjacent pieces and then keep looking until the image became clear. Furthermore, the resolution of most detective stories is condescending, no matter how ruthless the plotting, so that the reader, once the loose ends are tied up and the guilty finally punished, can return to the real world with the conviction that crimes get solved and remain locked between the covers of a book, that the world outside the book is guided by the same principles of justice as the tale told inside and should not be questioned.

19

Thinking about all that and going back to it during the following days and nights, lying in bed in a room that had been mine or sitting in a chair in the hallway of a hospital that was starting to feel familiar, in front of a round window into the room where my father was dying, I told myself that I had the material for a book and that this material had been given to me by my father, who had created a narrative in which I would have to be both the author and the reader, discovering as I narrated, and I wondered if my father had done it deliberately, if he had foreseen that one day he wouldn't be there to carry out the task himself and that this day was approaching, and he had wanted to leave a mystery as my inheritance; and I also wondered if he'd approve, as a journalist and therefore as someone who paid much more attention to the truth than I ever did. I've never felt comfortable with the truth. I had tried to stonewall it and give it the slip; I'd gone off to another country that hadn't been a reality for me from the very start, a place where the oppressive situation that was real to me for many years did not exist. I wondered, still and again, what my father would have thought of my writing a story I barely knew; I knew how it ended—it was obvious it ended in a hospital, as almost all stories do—but I didn't know how it began or what happened in the middle. What would my father think of my telling his story without understanding it completely, chasing after it in the stories of others as if I were the coyote and he the roadrunner and I had to resign myself to watching him fade into the horizon, leaving behind a cloud of dust, the wind taken out of my sails; what would my father think of my telling his story—the story of all of us—without really knowing the facts, with dozens of loose ends that I would knot up slowly to construct a narrative that stumbled along contrary to everything I'd set out to do, in spite of my being, inevitably, its author. What had my father been? What had he wanted? What was this backdrop of terror that I'd wanted to forget all about but that had come back to me when the pills ran out and I discovered the story of those disappearances, which my father had made his, which he'd explored as much as he could so he wouldn't have to venture into his own story?

20

The day after visiting the museum, I got sick. The first day, of course, was the worst; I remember the fever and the torpor and a series of dreams that repeated over and over again like a carousel whose operator had gone mad or was a sadist. Not all the dreams made sense, but their connecting thread did, and I remember what they said, even though it was fragmentary. In spite of my bad memory, in spite of the unfortunate series of circumstances that had made that memory worthless for a long period only just starting to come to an end, I can still to this day remember those dreams.

21

I dreamed that I went into a pet shop and stopped to look at the tropical fish; one of them in particular caught my eye: it was transparent, you could barely distinguish its silhouette from its transparent eyes and its organs; but, unlike the other fish, also somewhat clear, this one was completely crystalline and had its organs separated like colored rocks stuck inside it with no connection between them, a fistful of autonomous organs with no center of command.

22

I dreamed that I was writing in my old room in Göttingen and discovered insects in my pockets; I didn't know how they'd gotten there, and, although that would have been useful information, the only thing I was thinking about was making sure no one noticed that the insects were there, trying to get out.

22

I dreamed that I was riding a horse and its two front legs just came off while it drank water; the horse ate them, and then its head came off its neck and rolled around trying to reattach itself. I imagined that the horse would grow another head, first a stump like a fetus and then a head with a proper horse shape.

23

I dreamed that I was going up some stairs and three rings fell off my hands: the first was a silver ring in the shape of a zigzag that I wore on my index finger; the second was a ring in the shape of a chain, on my middle finger; the third was Ángela F.'s ring and it had a blue stone.

24

I dreamed that I was a boy and I was observing the preparations for what I understood to be a woman's suicide; the woman wore a housedress and lay in bed in what I recognized as a modest hotel room someplace in the Near East, with a rosary in her hands; on her bed was a white and red flag. The woman had a shotgun in her arms. She stared at me and I understood that she blamed me for what she was going to do. I'd thought the suicide would be fake, but in that moment I understood that it would be real. Before lifting the barrel of the shotgun to her mouth, she handed me a photograph that showed Juan Domingo Perón beside important members of the Peronist Resistance and she told me the photograph had been taken before they all started shooting each other. In the photograph I saw the woman.

22

I dreamed that I was dreaming about the relationship between the words *verschwunden* (disappeared) and *Wunden* (which doesn't exist independently in German but in certain cases is the plural of *Wund,* wound) and the words *verschweigen* (to keep quiet) and *verschreiben* (to prescribe).

11

I dreamed that I was back on the Argentine plain, watching a form of popular entertainment there called "off leash"; it involved tricking a monkey into getting into a well that was then filled with dirt, so that only the monkey's head could be seen. Then an animal, usually a lion, was released into the ring, and people bet on whether or not the monkey could escape from his trap and, if so, whether he could manage to kill the lion. The monkey pulled it off on very few occasions, but he always—

whether or not he defeated his opponent—ended up killing himself after seeing his similarity to the humans around him who took pleasure in such entertainment.

9

I dreamed that, on a train operated by the German company Metronom, I met a woman who was forced to carry a baby developing in a uterus located outside her body, tied to her only by the umbilical cord. If asked, the woman pulled the uterus out of a bag that she always had with her. The uterus was the size of a shoe; inside, the gestating baby displayed emotions and reactions that only the mother knew how to interpret. As the conductor approached, I asked her how to get to a town called Lemdorf or Levdorf, but she didn't answer. In the train station of an industrial city called Neustadt, whose smokestacks and factories could be seen from the station hall, the unresponsive conductor came over and told me I had two options for getting to Lemdorf or Levdorf: taking a bus that went halfway there and then taking another; or giving poisoned food to a beggar at the station door. Then I understood that Lemdorf or Levdorf, the place in northern Germany I was headed to, was hell.

26

I dreamed that I knew a method of divination: two people spit into each other's mouths; the transfer of liquid also transfers their plans and desires.

3

I dreamed that I was visiting Álvaro C. V. in a museum where he worked. The museum was located in a building reminiscent of the design school in Barcelona. I began to wander through its rooms, looking for Álvaro, and each room was different, all of them filled with objects that my attention seemed to want to settle on indefinitely. In one of them was a glass case displaying piston-like objects made of gourds that, according to the explanatory sign, produced sounds beyond all description. As I turned down a hallway, I finally found Álvaro and he and I went out, but my attention remained in the rooms and I understood that it wouldn't return to me until I had figured out what those devices were and could describe the sounds they produced. A moment later I was back in the museum, watching two experiments being carried out. In the first, a cat was submerged in a rubber solution and then mounted inside a cardboard tube. A woman explained that the result was an antenna that could be set up at home when the television or radio signal was too weak to be captured by a conventional antenna. Beside her, the cat still shook and meowed, but gradually stopped, since it couldn't breathe due to its cardboard corset, and finally its head fell slack while the antenna remained standing. Next, the experimenters grabbed a little monkey and put a cardboard collar on him similar to the ruffs worn in the seventeenth century. Then they started to cut the muscles below his neck, one by one, and studied how long they took to stop moving, analyzing how quickly the monkey understood what was happening to him, and conjecturing which muscles and veins to cut last to keep the animal alive as long as possible. I knew the cardboard collar had been placed on the monkey so that he wouldn't be terrified by the sight of what they were doing to him, but his timid moans, which devolved into mere gurgling, and the expressions on his face made me realize that he felt and knew perfectly what was happening. One by one his legs stopping moving, then his arms became stiff, his lungs stopped and, finally, when the animal's face was little more than a mask of horror, they cut a thick vein like a red thread that held together his head and the rest of his body beneath the cardboard collar and the monkey died.

22

I dreamed that I was watching television in a small hotel in Rome and that on the air they were talking about the wife of the Serbian prime minister Goran D. The woman's last name was "Cunt" and she was said to be in contact with the "vagina," or Russian mafia.

30

I dreamed that there was a crazy writer named Clara. A psychiatrist at her side supported her refusal to authorize an interview with a team of documentary filmmakers, and he said the word *humiliation* over and over again until she got up and put a white metal plate on her chair, saying that she was the plate. Then, using her fingernails, she wrote a physics formula on the cement floor and she left. In the following days she stopped eating. My theory was that the writer had wanted to express a desire, to ask for food, and she had done it the only way she knew how: as if we, wanting to eat watermelon, had asked for sugar and water. But the rest of the spectators thought that the physics formula—contrasting the sizes of the earth and the sun—could never be a request but was instead a revelation the writer was making to us before she died from starvation and firm resolve.

31

I dreamed that I was watching a film with my father. Some shoes, I think they were mine, lay on the floor between us and the television, which was showing a commercial made up of children's drawings of flying machines. A screen of handwritten text followed the commercial: We are all part of our language; when one of us dies, so does our name and a small but significant part of our native tongue. For this reason, because I don't want to impoverish the language, I have decided to live until the new words arrive. The signature at the end was illegible and only the three dates that followed it could be made out: 1977, 2008 and 2010. My father turned to me and said: 2010 is 2008 minus 1977, and 1977 is 2010 backward. You have nothing to fear. I replied: I'm not afraid, and my father turned his gaze back to the television screen and said: But I am.

IV

We are survivors, we outlive the deaths of others. There is nothing else to do. And there is nothing else to do but to inherit, whatever it may be. A house, a character, a society, a country, a language. Later others will arrive; we are also the people yet to come. What do we do with that inheritance?

—Marcelo Cohen

1

My mother's face was drawn together in a serious expression when I woke up, and she came over to me as if through the vibrant air of a summer day. Outside it was raining—it had started as I was returning from the museum the day before—and my mother's face seemed to sum up the absurd situation we were in: her husband and her son were sick and nobody knew what to do. As I always did when I was sick, I asked for my sister. She's at the hospital now, answered my mother, but she spent all day yesterday by your side. My mother put a damp cloth on my forehead. You went to the museum to see your father, she asked; she didn't wait for my reply. I figured, she said, and she turned her face away, which had already started to dampen with tears.

2

Outside the rain kept falling, and as it fell it seemed to swallow up the air, pushing it behind the solid curtain of water the rain formed between the sky and the earth, to a place where my lungs couldn't reach and neither could my parents' or my sister's. Although the air was filled with water, it also seemed empty, as if it hadn't really been replaced by water but rather by some intermediary substance, a substance of sadness and desperation and all the things you hope to never have to face, like the death of your parents, and yet are there the whole time, in a childish landscape of constant rain that you can't take your eyes off.

4

Is it morning or afternoon, I asked my brother when he appeared with a cup of tea. Afternoon, said my brother. Do you mean that it's after noon or truly the afternoon, I asked, but my brother had already left by the time I was able to articulate the question.

5

Is it morning or afternoon, I asked again. This time my brother was bringing me a bowl of soup that he'd made. It's night, he said, pointing outside. He told me that our mother and sister were at the hospital with our father and that they were going to spend the night there. So you're babysitting me, I said to him, trying to sound sarcastic. My brother answered: Let's watch TV, and he dragged over a small wheeled table with the television set on it.

6

I liked being there, with my brother. The fever had started to lift, but I still had problems focusing my vision for long periods and I had to look away when my brother started flipping through the local channels in search of a movie for us to watch. At one point he stopped on a show about policemen chasing criminals in a shantytown on the outskirts of the capital; the sound wasn't particularly good—it was recorded in the worst circumstances, in the midst of shoot-outs and wind and weather—and the local dialect seemed to have changed a lot since I'd left, so I didn't understand anything they were saying. The program had subtitles only when poor people were speaking, even though what the police said was incomprehensible too, and I thought for a moment about what kind of country this was in which the poor had to be subtitled, as if they were speaking a foreign language.

7

Finally my brother stopped on a channel where a movie was just starting. The premise was that a young man had suffered a minor accident and spent a few days in the hospital; on returning home, for some reason, he believed that his father was to blame for the accident and started to follow him, always keeping his distance. His father's behavior showed no signs of being dangerous, but, in the son's imagination, everything the father did was linked to a specific murder the son believed he was going to commit. If the father went into a store and tried on a jacket, the son thought he was planning to wear it as a disguise, since he never wore jackets like that. If his father flipped through a travel magazine in the barbershop, the son thought he was looking for a place to run off to after the murder. Because the son loved his father and didn't want him to end up in jail—and because he believed that he was the intended victim—he started to set traps to try to sabotage his father. He hid the jacket, burned his father's passport in the sink and destroyed his suitcases with a knife. For the father, these baffling domestic mishaps—his new jacket had disappeared, as had his passport; the suitcases he had in the house were torn—were surprising but also irritating. His usually jovial nature grew more and more bitter each day, and something inexplicable, something hard to justify but at the same time as real as an unexpected cloudburst, made him suspect that he was being followed. On his way to work, he obsessively searched the faces of his fellow passengers on the metro, and when he was out walking, he looked over his shoulder at every corner. He never saw his son, but his son saw him and attributed his nervousness and irritability to anxiety provoked by his imminent crime. One day the father told the son about his suspicion and the son tried to mollify him. Don't worry, it's just your imagination, he said, but the father was still jumpy. That same afternoon, tailing his father as he did every day, the son saw him buying a gun. When he got home that night, the father showed the weapon to his wife and son and they argued. The wife, who had doubted her husband's stability for some time, tried to snatch the gun away from him; there was a struggle that the son watched, speechless, until he let out a scream and forced himself between them. The gun went off and the mother fell down dead. Looking at her, the son realized that his intuition was both right and wrong: he had foreseen the crime but failed to see that he wouldn't be the victim, that he and not his father would commit the crime, that his father was nothing more than the instrument of someone else's runaway imagination. This all resulted from language, lost in a land that didn't belong to them. How can you *not* remember, she said. Back then journalists were getting killed by car bombs; he went out alone every day to start the car to protect us, to take on all the risk himself. I can't believe you don't remember, she said.

9

Then what I'd tried not to remember came back to me with unusual intensity, and it was no longer oblique, like the fuzzy images of photographs I'd been gathering just to have but not to look at. It came back head-on and with the overwhelming force of the fire truck I saw occasionally when I'd taken too many pills. It explained everything for me, explained the terror that I instinctively linked to the past, as if in the past we had lived in a country called fear with a flag that was a face filled with dread, explained my hatred toward the country of my childhood and my leaving that country, an exile that had begun long before I left for Germany and finally managed to forget everything. At one point I had wanted to believe that this voyage was a one-way trip, because I had no home to return to, given the conditions under which my family and I lived for a long time. But in that moment I realized I did have a home and that this home was a bunch of memories and those memories had always been with me, as if I were one of those stupid snails my grandfather and I used to torture when I was a boy.

10

When I was a boy, I had instructions not to bring other children home; if I had to walk down the street alone, I was supposed to walk against traffic and stay alert if a car stopped alongside me. I wore a card around my neck with my name, my age, my blood type and a contact telephone number: if someone tried to pull me into a car, I was supposed to throw that card to the ground and shout my name as loudly and as many times as I could. I wasn't allowed to stomp on the cardboard boxes I found on the street. I couldn't say a word about anything I ever heard at my house. In the house was an emblem painted by my father, two outstretched hands holding up something that looked like a hammer crowned by a Phrygian cap, with a background of sky blue and white, framed by a rising sun and some laurels; I knew it was the Peronist coat of arms but I couldn't mention it to anyone, and I was also supposed to forget what it meant. These rules, which I remembered for the first time in a long time, were designed to protect me, to protect my parents and my brother and sister and me in a time of terror, and though my parents may have already forgotten about them, I hadn't, because suddenly I thought of something that I still continued to do, even in Germany, when I was distracted: draw up imaginary routes to take me where I wanted to go, always walking against traffic.

11

About those snails: my grandfather and I would paint their shells different colors, and sometimes we'd write messages on them. Once, my grandfather left a greeting with his name and put the snail down on the ground. The snail left and a long time later some people brought it back to us: it had been found a few kilometers away, which was a significant distance for me but perhaps impossible for a snail; its feat made a real impression on me, and also left me thinking for a while that everything came back, that everything returned even if you were carrying all your possessions with you and had no reason to come back. Then I decided that I was never going to come back, and I kept that childhood promise to myself for a long time of German fog and medicated haze and, even though certain circumstances forced me to return, I hadn't returned to the country that my parents had wanted me to love, the one called Argentina, but rather to an imagined country, the one they had fought for and that had never existed. When I understood that, I also realized it hadn't been the pills that caused my inability to remember the events of my childhood, but rather those very events themselves that had provoked my desire to self-medicate and forget everything. And then I decided to remember, to do it for me and for my father and for what we'd both gone searching for, which had unintentionally reunited us.

12

My parents belonged to an organization called the Iron Guard. Unlike its unfortunate name, which links it to a Romanian organization from the period between the wars with which it has nothing else in common [1], my parents' organization was Peronist, though the philosophy of its members—moreover, of my parents [2]—seems to have been historical materialist [3] [4]. Given that most of its members did not come from Peronist homes, their efforts were geared toward finding out what it meant to be a Peronist, and they turned to the neighborhoods in which the grand Peronist narrative of the distribution of wealth and the times of prosperity and paternalism were still vivid in residents' memories, as was the presence of the Resistance [5], to which my parents' organization contributed in its last phase. This sets my parents' organization apart from the Montoneros, the organization it was, at one point, poised to merge with [6]: Iron Guard members didn't believe they possessed the truth of the revolutionary process but rather they went out to search for it in the lower classes' experience of resistance [7]; they didn't attempt to impose their practices but rather to acquire them. The other substantial difference was their rejection of violent methods; after a period of debate [8], the organization decided not to resort to weapons except for defensive means, and I suppose that's what saved the lives of my parents and a large number of their comrades and, indirectly, my own life [9]. From that moment on, the organization's main tools for building power were rhetoric and debate, whose potential for transformation is, as we all know, negligible; but something happened: for a long time they were the most powerful organization within Peronism and the only one with any real reach beyond the middle class, whose desire for transformation ended up proving nonexistent. Their objective was to create a "strategic rear-guard" [10], a state actually rooted in society, with the goals of replacing the militarized state, installed in 1955 and devoid of political legitimacy, and building power from the bottom up, dealing with real problems and avoiding violence except on the fringes in order to establish a legitimate alternative and as an element of agitation [11]. However, being a Peronist who was absolutely loyal to Perón had its pitfalls: unconditional adherence to the movement's leader led my parents' organization to accept an impotent government made up of an ignorant woman and a sadistic murderer nicknamed the Warlock because of his grotesque enthusiasm for the occult, and, furthermore, it led them down a dead end after Perón's death [12]. Where does an army go once its general is dead? Nowhere, obviously. Although Perón stated that his "only heir" was the people, who were in turn permeated by the Iron Guard, which swam among the people like a fish in water but at the same time gave them a channel and banks—as if the water had no meaning without the fish nor the fish without the water and one would disappear without the other—the Iron Guard dissolved after Perón's death [13], unable to take charge of a legacy that it would have to defend with weapons and bloodshed in the months to come. This also saved my parents' lives, and my life [14]. Those comrades who decided to join other organizations and continue their militancy were murdered and disappeared, others left the country, and the rest underwent a painful readjustment process, a sort of inner exile in which they had to witness the failure of a revolution definitively put down by the dictatorship. Those who continued or were ordered to continue were killed; my parents continued in their own way: my father stayed a journalist, as did my mother, and they had children to whom they passed on a legacy that is also a mandate, and that legacy and mandate—of social transformation and struggle—turned out to be unsuited to the times we grew up in, times of pride and frivolousness and defeat.

13

I was born in December 1975, which means I was conceived around March of that same year, slightly less than a year after the death of Perón and just a few months after the dissolution of the organization my parents were part of. I like to ask people I meet when they were born; if they are Argentines and were born in December 1975, I think we have something in common, since all of us born in that period are the consolation prizes our parents gave themselves after failing to pull off the revolution. Their failure gave life to us, but we also gave them something: in those years, a child was a good cover, a sign of a conventional life, far from revolutionary activities; a child could be, at a checkpoint or in a raid, the difference between life and death.

14

A minute. A minute was a lie, a cover story that my father and his coworkers were constantly inventing in case they were arrested; if the minute was good, if it was convincing, maybe they wouldn't be killed immediately. A good minute, a good story, was simple and brief but included superfluous details because life is full of them. Anyone who told his story from beginning to end was doomed because the ability to speak without hesitation—which is so rare in people—was, to their persecutors, much stronger evidence of the story's falseness than if it was about aliens or ghosts. In those days, a child was that minute.

15

Of course, a minute couldn't be told in a linear way, and I'm assuming my father had that in mind when he told me he would have liked to write a novel but not a straightforward one. I couldn't have been consistent with what my parents did and thought if I'd told his story that way; the question of how to narrate his story was equivalent to the question of how to remember it and how to remember them, and gave rise to other questions: how to describe what happened to my parents if they themselves hadn't been able to do so; how to tell a collective experience in an individual way; how to explain what happened to them without its looking like an attempt to turn them into the protagonists of a story that is collective; what place to occupy in that story.

16

In my parents' house I found some books on their organization, about which little has been written. In the days that followed, I read them in the hospital while I waited for someone to arrive with news, whether bad or good, and for that news to put an end to this period of uncertainty, this time outside of time that had begun its motionless voyage when my father got sick. In those books I discovered information I had only known in a vague way through what my parents had told me and through my own perception of fear. Here are the notes that flesh out what was written previously.

1. The Romanian Iron Guard was a religious organization on the extreme right of the political spectrum between the world wars and

deeply anti-Semitic; its founder was Corneliu Zelea Codreanu (9/13/1899–11/30/1938).

2. Actually, my parents came out of the National Student Front (FEN), which *was* a Marxist organization and converged with the orthodox Peronism of the Iron Guard in a coalition called the Single Organization for Generational Revitalization (OUTG), created in early 1972.

3. In practice, its leadership continued to be a paranoid Leninist minority.

4. In that sense, its enemies were humanists and Catholics, who are usually the correct enemies in all periods and circumstances.

5. The Resistance was a disjointed and plural movement that emerged spontaneously as an answer to Juan Domingo Perón's removal from power in June 1955 and his exile, the ban on his political party and the prohibition of the use of the name Perón and his image, as well as Peronist iconography in general. The methods of the Resistance were basically industrial sabotage, strikes and demonstrations; the most intense period of struggle was between the years 1955 and 1959, during which the movement came under the influence of John William Cooke.

6. An alliance between the Iron Guard and the Montoneros was discussed throughout 1971, and its main purpose was to endow the former with firepower and the latter with more influence and members: at its height, the Iron Guard had more than three thousand leaders and fifteen thousand mili-

tants and activists; my father was among the first group and my mother among the second, I believe.

7. Former members of the organization remember their main tasks as being agitation and propaganda in underprivileged neighborhoods, also at a school.

8. Apparently, the earliest members fantasized about the possibility of receiving military training in Algeria or Cuba but were dissuaded by Juan Domingo Perón himself.

9. Another difference between the two organizations: the leaders of the Iron Guard didn't abandon their followers or force them to die in the name of an idea they no longer believed in, as the Montoneros did after ordering a shift underground, leaving its militants unprotected, easy targets for their murderers.

10. On occasion this is also called a "strategic reserve of Peronism."

11. More specifically, their political project consisted of insinuating themselves into communities of Peronists (or *the people,* the term my parents preferred) once their political and revolutionary consciousness—which, according to the organization, already existed and therefore did not need to be taught—had been heightened.

12. One might say that its leadership hit a dead end long before, when reflection on the facts became more important than the facts themselves in the framework of the organization. In that sense, its role in Perón's

disastrous arrival at Ezeiza International Airport on June 20, 1973, presaged what would happen to the entire organization: caught between the Peronist right associated with unionism and the left represented by the Montoneros, it had to retreat.

13. The Iron Guard dissolved between July 1974 and March 1976; during that period, its leaders tried to preserve the institutional order but they were pragmatic, perhaps for the last time in their history, and worked under the assumption that there would be an imminent coup d'état, negotiating with the forces behind the coup for the protection of their members. Some remember that during the meeting in which the group was officially disbanded, the leaders asked for everyone's names and contact information; some even claim that those lists were given to the navy and that was what saved all their lives.

14. The organization's dissolution was an extraordinary event in the political life of Argentina, or any other country for that matter; it's difficult to imagine how an organization that, like this one, spent more than a decade—from 1961 to 1973—devoted to amassing power could then renounce that power following the death of its leader.

19

Among the things I was remembering were the stories my father's comrades told about the flurry of activity in the city of *osario during that period and how students and workers marched side by side in their demonstrations. Tapes of speeches by Juan Domingo Perón that he recorded in exile in Madrid and that periodically, through more or less mysterious channels, came into the hands of members of the organization, who spread them around the neighborhoods; by this I don't mean the content of the tapes—which I seem to remember my parents' comrades had forgotten—but rather their physicality, the tapes in their reels and the devices used to reproduce them, including one particular device that I used during my childhood and was black and white and often didn't work. A monument in the shape of an inverted spider that my parents and their comrades called the Mandarin, in a working-class neighborhood beside a stream of polluted water filled with prodigious fish. The stories of belonging to the organization, of its members' private lives, including the story of one comrade who had been expelled for having gone to bed with a member of a rival organization. The defections of some of its members, described with indignation but also with something like bafflement and compassion for their former comrades. A statistic—one hundred fifty members of the organization dead during the illegal crackdown—that had been determined by human rights organizations. My mother explaining to me one day how to create a barricade, how to unhitch a trolleybus and how to make a Molotov cocktail. The memory, real or imagined, of my father telling me that he had a press pass for the box where Perón was supposedly going to speak when he arrived at Ezeiza (this is the real part of the memory), and that, when the crossfire began, he hid behind the case of a double bass in the orchestra pit (in what might be the imagined part of the memory). Also my mother's stories about her march to meet Perón on his first return in 1972, her crossing the Matanza River with its thick rotten water up to her waist and some white pants she'd had to throw out, her stories and the stories of her girlfriends about Perón's death on July 1, 1974, and the lines to bid farewell to the great man in the cold driving rain that covered their tears, and the people approaching the young folks to give them food or a cup of coffee as they waited their turn out in the rain, more exposed to the elements than they'd ever been before; and later, the return by train, a train with broken windows that let in the cold and rain and all the death that would take place in the months and years to come; and the sadness and the crying and the feeling that every-ing my head whenever a police car passed, sharing the silence with my parents and my siblings, being somewhat perplexed every time that—but this happened many years later—my parents got together with their comrades and the painful memories and the happy ones were layered in their voices, along with the nicknames or noms de guerre that they still used, and got mixed up and melded into something difficult for me to explain and perhaps inconceivable to their children, and that was an affection and a solidarity and a loyalty among them that went beyond the differences they might have had in the present and which I attributed to a feeling that I too could have had toward other people if we'd shared something unique and fundamental, if—and this, of course, sounds childish or perhaps metaphorical, but it's not in the least—I'd been willing to give my life for people and those people had been willing to give their lives for me.

20

There was also a phrase that stood out against a distinctive profile, a profile every Argentine knows because it is Juan Domingo Perón's profile. That profile is beloved or despised, but it could replace the drawings of the fatherland they made us do in school as one of the most recognizable symbols of

Argentina; the phrase was a quote by Perón himself, and its presence in my parents' living room made it sacred and forced us to memorize it. I still haven't forgotten it: "As a man of destiny I believe that no one can escape it. However, I believe that we can help it along, strengthen it, and turn it in our favor until it becomes synonymous with victory."

21

What could I do with that mandate? What could my brother and sister do with it, and what about all the others I would later meet, the children of militants in my parents' organization but also those of members of other organizations, all lost in a world of dispossession and frivolity, all members of an army defeated long ago whose battles we can't even remember and our fathers don't even dare to face? The Greek historian Xenophon told the history of an army like that, some ten thousand Greek soldiers who failed in their attempt to install Cyrus the Younger on the Persian throne and so were forced to cross almost four thousand kilometers of enemy territory before reaching the refuge of the Greek colony of Trabzon. The march described by Xenophon, one of the most terrible in history, lasted barely a year, but to understand the true dimensions of what happened to us I would have to imagine that it lasted several dozen years, and I would have to think of those soldiers' children, raised among the instruments of a defeated army who had crossed the deserts and snowy mountain caps of a hostile territory, burdened with the inevitable weight of defeat and without even the comfort of the memory of a period in which defeat wasn't imminent and everything was still to come. When they reached Trabzon, the ten thousand soldiers Xenophon told of were barely half their number, just five thousand men.

22

I wondered what my generation could offer that could match the exuberant desperation and thirst for justice of the preceding generation, our parents'. Wasn't it a terrible ethical imperative that generation unintentionally imposed on us? How do you kill your father if he's already dead, and in many cases died defending an idea that seems noble even if its execution was remiss or clumsy or wrongheaded? How else could we measure up if not by doing as they did, fighting a senseless war that was lost before it began and marching into slaughter to the sacrificial chants of disaffected youth, arrogant and impotent and stupid, marching to the brink of civil war against the forces of the repressive machinery of a country that, in essence, is and always has been conservative? Something had happened to my parents and to me and to my siblings that prevented me from ever knowing what a home was or even what a family was, though everything seemed to indicate I had both. Once, my parents and I had an accident that I wasn't able to or hadn't wanted to remember: something crossed our path and our car spun around a few times and went off the highway, and we were now wandering through the fields, our minds blank, that shared experience the only thing uniting us. Behind us there was an overturned car in a ditch on the side of a country road, bloodstains on the seats and in the grass and on our clothes, but none of us wanted to turn around and look back, even though that was what we had to do and that was what I was trying to do as I held my father's hand in a hospital in the provinces.

24

A conversation one night with my sister, in the hospital: I asked her about the names I'd found on a list among my father's papers, the names of those who had participated in that first newspaper he'd started, and what Alicia Burdisso was doing there. Those are names of people from the town, answered my sister; many of them were politically active and one of them was Alicia. Then I said: That's why he was searching for her, after so long; because he'd gotten her into politics and he was still alive and she was dead. My sister laid her hand on my shoulder, and then she went to the end of the hallway, where I could no longer see her.

27

In one of my parents' books I found some passages about the last place Alicia Burdisso had been seen alive. My father had underlined, in pencil and in a trembling hand:

> Central Police Headquarters, Radio Patrol Command, Firemen's Barracks and the School of Physical Education, all located in the capital of the province [of Tucumán]. La Compañía de Arsenales "Miguel de Azcué-naga," El Reformatorio and El Motel on the outskirts. Nueva Baviera, Lules and Fronte-rita in various locations in the interior. [...] double barbed-wire fence, guards with dogs, heliports, surveillance towers, et cetera. [...] The detainees who passed through those places mostly did so for short periods, and were later transferred. There is a serious possibility that, in many cases, the transfer

culminated with the prisoners' murder. "The prisoners were taken to the 'Escuelita' in private cars either in the trunk, in the backseat or lying on the floor. Then the prisoners were taken out, and from the little we knew, when that happened, most of them were executed. If a detainee died, they waited for nightfall, and after wrapping the body in an army blanket, they stuck it into one of the private cars that were headed who knows where" (from the testimony of Officer Antonio Cruz, Dossier 4636). "They put a red ribbon around the necks of those sentenced to death. Every night a truck picked them up to take them to the extermination camp" (from the testimony of Fermín Núñez, Dossier 3185). [. . .] Right in the center of the city of San Miguel, the Central Police Headquarters, which was already functioning as a torture center, became [. . .] a Clandestine Detention Center. In that period Lieutenant Colonel Mario Albino Zimermann was the Chief of Police in Tucumán [. . .]. He was joined by Commissioner-Inspector Roberto Heriberto Albornoz [. . .] and Captains José Bulacio [. . .] and David Ferro [. . .]. The army maintained control of this place through a military supervisor. The person in charge of Security Area 321, Lieutenant Colonel Antonio Arrechea, of the 5th Brigade, would visit the center and attend torture sessions [. . .]. The neighbors heard the moans and screams of the victims and, often, shots fired in bursts that were either simulated executions by firing squad or, simply, executions.

28

In one of those centers, at the Central Police Headquarters, Alicia Burdisso had last been seen, and my father had underlined her name with red ink that made a mark like a scar or a wound.

30

When I read this, I understood that my dream had been a warning or a reminder for my father and for me, and that in it the transformation of the word *verschwunden* (disappeared) into *Wunden* (wounds) was related to what had happened to my father, and the transformation of the word *verschweigen* (to keep quiet) into *verschreiben* (to prescribe) had to do with what had happened to me, and I thought the moment had come to put an end to it all. As the pills dissolved slowly in the toilet bowl and began to transport their message of unwarranted happiness to fish who would receive it with their little open mouths at the end of the network of sewers that led to the river, I thought

I would have to talk to my father, if that was possible someday, and resolve all my questions, and that task, the task of finding out who my father had been, would keep me busy for a long time, maybe until I was a father myself someday, and no pill could do it for me. I also understood that I had to write about him and that writing about him was going to mean not only finding out who he had been, but also, and above all, finding out how to write about one's father, how to be a detective and gather the information available but not judge him, and give all that information to an impartial judge whom I didn't know and perhaps never would know. I thought of the unfortunately apt parable of the fate of the disappeared, of their family members and of their attempts to repair something that couldn't be repaired, which brought yet another symmetry to this story of a missing brother and a missing sister: my father and I were searching for a person, I for my father and he for Alberto Burdisso but also, and above all, for Alicia Burdisso, who had been his friend as a teenager and who, like him, became politically active in that period and was a journalist, but died. My father had started to search for his lost friend and I, without meaning to, had also started shortly afterward to search for my father. This was our lot as Argentines. And I wondered whether this could also be a political task, one of the few with relevance for my own generation, which had believed in the liberal project that led a large portion of the Argentine people into poverty in the 1990s and made them speak an incomprehensible language that had to be subtitled; a generation, as I was saying, that had gotten burned, but some of us still couldn't forget. Someone once said that my generation would be the rear guard of the young people in the 1970s who'd fought a war and lost it, and I also thought about that mandate and how to carry it out, and I thought a good way would be to one day write about everything that had happened to my parents and me and hope that others would feel compelled to start their own inquiries into a time that still hasn't ended for some of us.

31

One day I got a call from the university where I worked back in Germany. A female voice, which I imagined emerging from a straight neck extending down from a small chin to a slightly open shirt collar, in a small office filled with plants and smelling of coffee and old paper, since all German offices are like that, told me that I had to come back to work or they would be forced to terminate my contract. I asked her for a few days to think it over, and I heard the echo of my voice down the telephone line, speaking in a foreign language. The woman agreed and hung up. I had two days to decide what to do, but I also realized there was no need to think it over: I was there and I had a story to write and it would make a good book because it had a mystery and a hero, pursuer and pursued, and I had already written stories like that and knew I could do it again; however, I also knew this story had to be told in a different way, in fragments, in whispers and with laughter and with tears, and I knew I would be able to write it only once it became part of the memories I'd decided to recover, for me and for them and for those who would follow. As I thought all this, standing beside the telephone, I noticed it had started to rain again, and I told myself I would write that story because what my parents and their comrades had done didn't deserve to be forgotten, and because I was the product of what they had done, and because what they'd done was worthy of being told because their ghost—not the right or wrong decisions my parents and their comrades had made but their spirit itself—was going to keep climbing in the rain until it took the heavens by storm.

32

Someone once said there's a minute that escapes the clock so it never has to happen and that minute is the minute in which someone dies; no minute wants to be that moment, and it flees and leaves the clock gesticulating with its hands and an idiot's face.

33

Perhaps it was that, perhaps it was the unwillingness of a minute to be the minute in which someone stops breathing, but the fact is my father didn't die: in the end, something made him cling to life and he opened his eyes and I was there when he did it. I think he wanted to say something, but I warned him: You have a tube in your throat, you can't speak, and he looked at me and then he closed his eyes and he seemed, finally, to rest.

35

The last time I was in the hospital, my father still wasn't able to speak, but he was conscious and his pulse had stabilized and it looked like he would soon be breathing again without the help of a machine. My mother left us alone and I thought I needed to tell him something, I needed to tell him what I'd discovered about his search for the disappeared siblings and what that had led me to remember and how I'd decided to start to remember there and then, willing to recover a history that belonged to him and to his comrades and also to me, but I didn't know how to do it. Then I remembered I was carrying a book with me and I began to read to him; it was a book of poems by Dylan Thomas, and I read until the light coming through the window of that hospital room had faded completely. When that happened, I thought I'd be able to cry in the darkness without my father seeing, so I did, for a long while. I don't know if my father did as well. In the darkness, I could make out only his motionless body in the bed and his hand, to which I was clinging. When I could speak again, I told him: Hold on, you and I have to talk, but now you can't and I can't; someday, though, maybe we can, like this or some other way, and you have to hold on until that day comes. Then I let go of his hand and I left the room and I continued crying for a while in the hallway.

36

That night, before I caught my plane, my mother and I looked at some photographs my father had taken of me with his Polaroid camera when I was a boy. In them I was faded; soon my past would be having done all that. Your father wouldn't have minded that his comrades had lived only to betray the revolution and its ideals, which is what we all do by living, because living is very much like having a plan and doing your best to keep it from succeeding, but his comrades, our comrades, didn't have time. Your father would have liked for the bullets that killed them to have given them time to live and to leave behind children who wanted to understand and would try to understand who their parents had been and what they'd done and what had been done to them and why they were still alive. Your father would have liked for our comrades to have died that way instead of being tortured, raped, murdered, thrown from airplanes, drowned in the sea, shot in the neck, in the back, in the head, with their eyes open, looking toward the future. Your father would have liked not to be one of the few who survived, because a survivor is the loneliest person in the world. Your father wouldn't have minded dying if in exchange there was a possibility that someone would remember him and later decide to tell his story and the story of his comrades who marched with him to the goddamn end of the story. Perhaps he thought, as he sometimes did: "At least it's in writing," and that whatever was in writing would be a mystery and would make my son search for his father and find him, and also find those who shared with his father an idea that could only end badly. That in searching for his father he would understand what happened to him and to those he loved and why all that makes him who he is. That my son knows, in spite of all the misunderstandings and the defeats, there is a struggle and it goes on, and that struggle is for truth and justice and light for those who are in darkness. That's what my mother said just before closing the photo album.

40

Sometimes I still dream of my father and my siblings: the fire truck passes by on its way to hell, and I think about those dreams and write them down in a notebook and they remain there, like photographs from the birthday when I turned seven and laughed with a laugh missing two or three teeth and that absence was the promise of a better future for us all. Sometimes I also think that perhaps I can never tell this story but I should try anyway, and I also think that even though the story as I know it may be inaccurate or false, its right to exist is guaranteed by the fact that it is also my story and by the fact that my parents and some of their comrades are still alive: if that's true, if I don't know how to tell the story, I should do it anyway so that they feel compelled to correct me in their own words, so that they say the words that as their children we have never heard but that we need to unravel to complete their legacy.

41

Once, my father and I went deep into the woods and my father began to teach me how to find my way by observing the location of moss on tree trunks and the position of certain stars; we were carrying ropes and he tried to show me how to knot them to the trunks and use them to climb or descend a slope; he also explained how to camouflage myself, how to quickly find a hiding spot and how to move through the woods without being seen. At the time, these lessons didn't interest me much, but they came back to me when I closed my father's file. In that moment, it seemed like what my father had wanted to teach me that day, in that absurd game of guerrillas I unwittingly found myself involved in, was how to survive, and I wondered if that wasn't the only thing he'd ever tried to teach me over the years. My father had seen in me a sickly and possibly defenseless boy, maybe just as he himself was in his childhood, and he tried to toughen me up by showing me the most brutal side of nature, which is fundamentally tragic; so, during our visits to the countryside, I witnessed the slaughter of cows, hens and horses whose deaths were part of life in the country but in me left an indelible footprint of fear. This display of the world's brutality and of the infinitesimal distance separating life and death didn't make me stronger; rather, it crippled me with an indefinable terror that has accompanied me ever since. However, perhaps confronting me with terror was my father's chosen method of saving me from experiencing it, perhaps the display was meant to make me indifferent to it or, alternatively, aware enough of it to learn to watch out for myself. Sometimes I also think about my father beside the well where Alberto José Burdisso was found, and I imagine myself standing next to him. My father and I amid the ruins of a house some three hundred meters from an isolated country road, barely some walls and some mounds of brick and rubble among the chinaberry trees and wild privet and weeds, both of us contemplating the black mouth of the well in which lie all the dead of Argentine history: all the defenseless and underprivileged; those who died trying to oppose a deeply unjust violence with a possibly just violence; and all those killed by the Argentine state, the government that rules over a land where only the dead bury the dead. Sometimes I remember wandering with my father through a forest of low trees, and I think that forest is the forest of fear, and he and I are still in there, and he keeps guiding me, and perhaps we'll get out of the woods someday.

EPILOGUE

In the time since the events narrated in this book took place, there have been several new pieces of information regarding the fates of Alicia Raquel Burdisso and her brother, Alberto José Burdisso. On June 19, 2010, *La Capital de *osario* published the news that the Sixth Sentencing Court of the province of Santa Fe condemned Gisela Córdoba and Marcos Brochero to twenty years in prison for willful and premeditated homicide, and Juan Huck to seven years in prison for voluntary manslaughter. According to Marcelo Castaños and Luis Emilio Blanco, the authors of the article, the courts determined the facts as follows:

> Shortly after dawn on the first Sunday of June, Gisela Córdoba, 27 years old at the time, set out for the countryside along with Brochero, 32 (her husband), Burdisso and Huck, 61 years old. They traveled in a blue Peugeot 504 to a house in ruins located roughly eight kilometers from the city center. The pretext was collecting firewood for a barbecue, something they did with some frequency.
>
> [. . .] The courts later determined that

on that morning, when passing by the well, Burdisso was pushed in, fell 12 meters and hit the bottom, breaking five ribs and one shoulder, dislocating the other. According to the autopsy, the victim remained there wounded for three days until Brochero returned to the scene, and after seeing that Burdisso was still alive, he broke stones from the well and threw the rubble in, along with dirt, construction materials, corrugated metal sheets and branches.

"He buried him alive. It was gruesome because the man had dirt in his mouth and respiratory tract, which is to say that he tried to breathe under the material thrown onto him," a court source recently commented. The autopsy indicated "death by suffocation due to confinement."

[. . .] The couple now sentenced had been taking advantage of the man from El Trébol for some time. Córdoba pretended to be in a relationship with him and had gotten most of a reparation of more than 200 thousand pesos that the victim had received.

Under false pretenses she gradually took possession of the proceeds from the sale of Burdisso's house and car. She also took the furniture, electrical appliances and a large part of the salary he received as an employee at the Club Trebolense. [. . .] A week prior to his disappearance, Córdoba offered to rent the house to a man with the nickname of The Uruguayan. [. . .] The same day of the disappearance, Córdoba showed the house to The Uruguayan and afterward they signed a lease.

She also believed herself to be the beneficiary of a life insurance policy Burdisso had, and therefore, after having murdered him, she asked Huck to take him out of the well and throw him somewhere where they could find him and confirm his death so that she could demand compensation. Huck did not comply with her request.

The homicide hearing [heard by Eladio García, Judge of the Court of First Instance for the Investigation of Criminal and Correctional Affairs in San Jorge] lasted until September 2008. In the meantime, 17 people were arrested, the rest of whom were released, leaving the three accused. [. . .]

*

The fate of Alicia Raquel Burdisso is, like that of thousands of disappeared people during the most recent Argentine dictatorship, much more difficult to establish, but her name was mentioned again, this time by one of the witnesses at the trial of dictator Luciano Benjamín Menéndez, held at the Federal Oral Tribunal (TOF) in Tucumán, who stated that he saw her in the Clandestine Detention Center run out of the Police Headquarters in San Miguel de Tucumán; his testimony was based on lists of detainees made in 1977 by the Tucumán Police Intelligence—headed by

Menéndez—which showed the fate of each victim. Alicia Burdisso was murdered at that Police Headquarters that year. In the trial, sentences were handed down for the former chief of police in Tucumán, Roberto Heriberto "One-Eye" Albornoz, life without parole; former policeman Luis de Cándido, held accountable for aggravated illicit association, home invasion, illegitimate deprivation of liberty and usurpation of real property and sentenced to eighteen years of prison; his brother Carlos, who received a suspended sentence of three years for having seized a house belonging to one of the victims; and Menéndez himself, who received a life sentence—the fourth such sentence he had gotten by that point—for "crimes of home invasion, aggravated illegitimate deprivation of liberty, aggravated torture, torture leading to death and premediated homicide." The trial had also begun for the former governor Antonio Domingo Bussi (eighty-four), who was declared unfit for trial due to health reasons, while two of the accused military men, Albino Mario Zimmerman (seventy-six) and Alberto Cattáneo (eighty-one), died in March and May 2010, which speaks to the urgency with which these trials—and the private trials, the task of finding out who those who came before us were, which is the subject of this book—must be carried out.

*

While the events told in this book are mostly true, some are the result of the demands of fiction, whose rules are different from the rules of such genres as testimony or autobiography; for that reason I would like to mention here what the Spanish writer Antonio Muñoz Molina once said, as a reminder and a warning: "A drop of fiction taints everything as fictional." When my father read the manuscript of this book, he thought it was important to make some observations that reflect his perspective on the narrated events and correct certain errors; the text that gathers these observations, and which is the first example of the type of reactions this book is intended to provoke, can be found at http://patriciopron.blogspot.com/p/el-espiritu-de-mis-padres-sigue.html under the title "The Record Straight."

∗

I would like to thank here those people who have supported and encouraged the writing of this book and the authors whose works have been points of reference and inspiration for me, particularly Eduardo De Grazia. I would also like to thank Mónica Carmona and Claudio López Lamadrid, my editors at Random House Mondadori, and Rodrigo Fresán, Alan Pauls, Miguel Aguilar, Virginia Fernández, Eva Cuenca, Carlota del Amo and Alfonso Monteserín; also Andrés "Polaco"

Patricio Pron, born in 1975, is the author of three story collections and four previous novels. His work has received numerous prizes, including the Juan Rulfo Short Story Prize and the Jaén Novel Prize. He lives in Madrid, where he works as a translator and critic.

A NOTE ON THE TYPE

This book was set in Fairfield, a typeface designed
by the distinguished American artist and engraver
Rudolph Ruzicka (1883–1978). In its structure Fairfield displays the sober and sane qualities of the
master craftsman whose talents were dedicated
to clarity.

Typeset by Scribe, Philadelphia, Pennsylvania
Printed and bound by RR Donnelley,
Harrisonburg, Virginia
Designed by Robert C. Olsson